From the Mallee

Colin Rogers

From the Mallee

Five Stories

From the Mallee: Five Stories
ISBN 978 1 76041 707 9
Copyright © Colin Rogers 2019

First published 2019 by
GINNINDERRA PRESS
PO Box 3461 Port Adelaide 5015
www.ginninderrapress.com.au

Contents

The Ute

She struggles to identify the noise that had woken her. It couldn't have been terribly loud, just a brief inconsistency in the background murmur that had lulled her to sleep. A comforting blend of warm breezes through the wisteria, the hum of refrigerator, her own breathing.

But something had snapped her to instant awareness. One of those ancestral reactions that remind us that we're not so far removed from our caves.

Now she lies stock-still, her pulse amplified inside her head by a damp pillow, her breathing far too loud. She concentrates her senses within the room.

Nothing…no presence. None of that sense of a space filled by something unknown.

She listens beyond the room, seeking the brush of an elbow against the passage wall, the muffled complaint of floorboard buried below strata of old lino.

Still nothing.

Outside perhaps? Her half-opened window admits a summer zephyr scented with eucalyptus and warm dust.

She pictures the backyard. The patch of neglected vegetables that never stood a chance against the chooks or the invading couch grass, untended fruit trees that support only occasional possum wars and the galvo shed that hides the optimistically named lawnmower. The washing line stretching from the veranda to the peppercorn with a single centre pole to push the line higher and stop the sheets from dragging through the dust or the mud.

Down in the back corner, next to the shed, the battered old Chevy ute. One of the Yanks' lend-lease trucks. Well, the Yanks called them trucks but it was really nothing more than half-ton ute. He'd brought it back with him when he was demobbed. Told her that he'd bought it at a surplus sale with his payout. Most of the locals reckoned otherwise, reckoned that he'd probably flogged it and driven it back from Alice Springs. There was a lot of pilfering going on after the Jap surrender. Lots of perfectly good military stuff lying around, unaccounted for, just begging for some enterprising ex-soldier to supplement his army payout. One of the few perks of the job.

There was a good yarn going around about a digger who hadn't waited for the surrender. He'd driven his fully laden semi out of the Alice Springs compound and, instead of heading north to Darwin, he'd aimed it south with the intention of flogging the lot in Adelaide. They'd caught him just short of Port Augusta. Threw the book at him: desertion, major larceny, impeding the war effort, everything they could think of. The poor bugger is probably still watching the world through prison bars.

She smiled to herself in the dark, remembering the front-page story. The authorities had wanted to make an example of that digger... painted him as a traitor. Somehow the public got it all wrong and hailed him as something between a Robin Hood and a Ned Kelly. If anything, it only encouraged the pilfering and petty thieving.

It was amusing at the time, but, thinking back, a lot of their problems had started with that bloody ute. There were a few blokes in the RSL who reckoned that driving trucks up to Darwin didn't count as real war service. These blokes had been in the furnace of North Africa or the suffocation of New Guinea: the mud, the bugs, the rot. They'd seen the worst of war. Some of them had lost mates. Some of them had come back all emaciated and ulcerated and a bit frightening. And a few of them didn't want to drink with a bloke who had spent the whole war sitting behind the wheel of a Yank truck trundling between The Alice and Darwin. A bloke who had never seen a Kraut or a Dago or a Jap. A bloke who had never fired a gun and never been shot at, never went hungry. Always onto the perks. Not many perks in El Alamein or on the Kokoda.

But she had known none of this back then. All she saw was a good-looking, healthy young bloke with a big grin and a decent sort of ute.

Again, she smiled to herself as the good memories played themselves across the theatre of her mind. She was a bit of a looker back then. Even today she still scrubbed up pretty well, truth be known. Bearing the twins and then eight years of child-rearing hadn't turned her into one of those lumpy frumps that she encountered every day when she walked the boys to school. So she could still pull an admiring glance from the local blokes.

Not that she had any interest in many of them. Mostly a bunch of no-hopers. Born in the mallee, grew up in the mallee, worked in the mallee. Dumb as stumps. One or two were maybe worth a second look. Lachlan James, the local copper, for one. She'd seen a lot of him when things went really bad and, since then, she seemed to be always bumping into him. She liked the way that he insisted on being called Lachlan and not Locky or Jamesy. Not a bad-looking bloke either. Good prospects. Fitted in pretty well with the locals but likely to be transferred out of the mallee and on to the Big Smoke anytime. So, not much chance of hooking up with him. She'd never leave this place, never be able to leave the ute.

So there it sat. Front end all smashed up, tyres flat and sitting on the rims. Going nowhere. A couple of the locals had offered to buy it, to fix it up enough to use out on their farms or to salvage spare parts. She'd told them that her boys would raise merry hell if she ever got rid of it. It was their favourite plaything. They spent hours propped up behind the wheel making long raspberry noises that were supposed to sound like the roar of the engine but really sounded like endless farts. Sometimes it was a cop car, sometimes it was Fangio at Monza, or was it Moss at Silverstone? She wasn't up on her grand prix and didn't know where the boys got their know-how about international motor sport.

Probably from school. It never ceased to amaze her what they picked up at school, and only about half of it from the teacher.

He'd be a good catch, that teacher: Mister Morris. She thought that his first name was Richard but everyone, even the mums, only ever called him Mister Morris. But, like the copper, Mister Morris was destined to move on. And she was destined to stay here, in the mallee. Her and the ute.

Anyway, the boys prefer the busted-up Chevy to the garish swing-see-saw that was the big event of last Christmas. Ironic that: they're happy to play on the wreck that caused so much infuriation but they hardly go near the expensive plaything that he'd bought for them last Christmas. As if they were rejecting his gift just like he'd rejected them. Through the eyes of children, she thought. Thank Christ they hadn't seen the rest of it.

She'd kicked off the sheet but it was still too hot. Sliding off the bed, she crept to the window and eased the sash up a couple of inches. Still careful not to make a sound, still worried by whatever had woken her. The faint breeze caressed her nightie with a delicious coolness so she leaned forward, hands on the sill, and shook out her dampened hair.

The lopsided Chevy grille grinned at her from between the shed and the peppercorn.

'Yes,' she pondered. 'There's a bigger irony there than anyone would guess at. That bloody ute won't be going anywhere. It'll never move from that spot.' She'd make sure of that.

They'd married within six months of his return from the Territory and they'd driven the Chevy ute over to Sydney for their honeymoon. She was pregnant with the twins within the following six months.

He'd qualified for a war service home loan and they'd bought this fibro and corro place on the edge of town, almost in the mallee. Close enough to walk to the shops but far enough away from neighbours.

She liked the mallee. When he was off at work and before the boys were born, she'd often walk through it alone. She liked the intimacy of it, how you can't see any horizons and how it crowds in on you subtly. The trees' multi-trunks cast dark shadows on the sandy ground so that the isolated open spaces are barred like small prison exercise yards.

He was a good worker back then, good with his hands. Laying bricks, bush carpentry, fencing. Good with cars and most things mechanical, so he soon found steady work in the one-and-only garage.

The scornful blokes in the RSL had relented a bit when he described his near-misses when the Japs bombed Darwin. Twice he'd been in the thick of it. Three times if you counted both raids on that first day. Sheltering under the truck as the bombs plastered the place and then pitching in to help pull survivors from the debris.

He'd been down on the docks when the *Neptuna* blew up and he'd helped pull some of the survivors out of the water. Not many, though; thirty-six blokes died.

A lot of diggers didn't talk about their war experiences. But he did. Couldn't shut him up once he got started and once he'd got a couple under his belt. Turned out that it was his dodgy knee that had kept him off the front line, an old footy injury that flared up every now and then. He'd tried to join the infantry but they'd knocked him back. He'd been lucky to get into the transport division. He'd done his stuff all right, pulled his weight. Kept the supply lines open. Must have driven them bloody trucks a million miles, crook knee and all.

It was a ferrety little bugger called Lou who stuffed things up. He was one of a small army of ex-diggers who hadn't done so well since the demob. It was a bit like the old days of swaggies on the wallaby. Homeless blokes who drifted into town, maybe picked up a bit of work and then just faded back into the mallee.

One or two of them might wander into the RSL of a Friday night. Fridays were the only days that they opened the little bar at the back of the RSL hall, where the transients could be sure of a complimentary beer and a yarn. Perhaps pick up news of a spot of work in the offing.

Lou had spent time at the Alice Springs supply depot. He was a despatch orderly, so he knew all of the truck drivers. More to the point, he knew who had never driven a truck to Darwin and who had never been in Darwin during the raids and who had never pulled survivors of the *Neptuna* from the water.

'Footy injury?' scoffed Lou. 'Nah, not if we're talking about the same bloke. Crook knee? Nah…told us he had a crook back. Something about a branch falling on him while he was saving someone from a bushfire. Reckoned he couldn't sit behind the wheel of a truck for more than half an hour, so he was confined to light duties around the depot. Spent more time nicking stuff than he did loading trucks. A real bludger.'

Another noise snapped her back from her preoccupation. A series of sharp, staccato cracks. Just the corro roof cooling off a bit. These fibro and corro hot-boxes went off like a machine gun whenever they warmed up or cooled down.

No, it was a different noise that had woken her. But she couldn't hear it now.

The breeze was picking up and the moon shadows were dancing over the baked earth and desiccated couch grass. The peppercorn flicked its shadow across the front of the ute, picking out those bits of chrome that hadn't flaked off and those bits of glass that hadn't busted. First one headlight and then the other flickered silver in the reflected moonlight as if it was winking at her, sharing the secret.

The flurries took hold of the swing. The first time it had moved in weeks. You couldn't do much on a swing. Just…swing. Back and forth. It never became a cop car or a grand prix racer. It was pretty much useless, just like their father.

She hated it and the twins hardly ever played on it. She ought to have dragged it out into the scrub months ago and left it to rust. But word gets around. Dumping the swing, the only thing that he had ever bought for his sons, might be a signal to the whole town. Might expose the depths of her hatred for the man, might raise suspicions. This place thrived on gossip. Those lumpy-frumps would have a field day. They'd make sure that their brats heard the dinner-table gossip and took it to the schoolyard. The twins would probably be told that their mother was a bitch even if they weren't old enough to understand the word. Just as they hadn't been old enough to sense the veiled hostilities that passed between their parents for so long.

The ute and the swing. Both, in different ways, menacing reminders of the bad time. Metaphors for the endless silent skirmish that had become their marriage.

The truth about his army service had ripped through town like a plague and he became an instant pariah. You can get away with a fair bit of bullshit in a country town but you never, never skite about your time in the army. He was a bullshit artist and a liar. There was no place for him at the RSL bar of a Friday night. He drank in the pub and he usually found himself drinking alone until one or two of the town's more unsavoury types got half-pissed and didn't care who they drank with.

So he lost his job. Well, he told anyone who would listen that he'd lost his job. But everyone knew that he'd got the shove. Too often late, too often hungover, too unreliable, Too contemptible.

She'd kept on at the bakery, mostly serving customers and keeping the shopfront looking clean and tidy. Trev's a good baker and a good bloke and his missus, Barb, is really struggling with her crook hip so she can't spend long on her feet. She mostly did the books and the fancy decorations on the special orders. Trev and Barb knew what was going on. Gave her a few extra hours whenever they could.

It came as a bit of a surprise when the lumpy-frumps didn't get stuck into her. Nor did their brats give the twins any lip at school. In fact, she found herself getting nods and brief smiles from some of the most vicious gossips in town. She figured out that his crime, his deceit, had been just too outrageous. No one could hold her liable of guilt by association. He'd lied to the town and he'd lied to her. All the heroic stories about the Darwin bombings had been bullshit. And he'd been spinning them for years. To her, his wife, and his kids.

Life became shit. They hardly ever spoke. They hardly ever found themselves in the same room. They'd kept the hostilities simmering quietly. She was anxious to shield the boys from his drunkenness and her humiliation. Everything about their marriage had been revealed as a sham, a deception. She had never hurt so much.

He'd still be asleep when she took the boys to school and then walked on to the bakery. Then she'd get home and find that he'd left all the housework for her to sort out and he'd be down at the pub.

So the boys hardly ever saw him. It didn't seem to worry them. It came as a jolt to realise that she'd never noticed how little they cared for their father. He'd never kicked a footy with them, never bowled a ball or shown them how to use a hammer.

If it hadn't been for the twins, she would have just walked away and left him to self-destruct.

Most nights she'd cry herself to sleep and then immediately wake up and rage against herself for her weakness. Then she'd hear the Chevy come howling down the road in the wrong gear. Sometimes he'd manage to find the back door. More often than not he'd sleep in the ute.

It was only a matter of time before he did something really stupid. She knew something was wrong when she heard him creep the ute up the drive instead of flogging it like he usually did. She got out of bed and pulled on a dressing gown. It was raining quite heavily but she could still hear giggling in the backyard. Blokes giggling, like they did when they were pissed.

He and one of his dumb pub maggots were draped over the bonnet and laughing like girls in the rain. And the ute was a mess. The grill was all pushed in and one front wheel was angled all wrong. The whole vehicle looked to be sagging on its front suspension.

She'd screamed from the veranda as she pulled on her boots. 'What the hell have you done? What did you hit?'

The pub maggot, she thought that it was the one called Pozzer, snorted. 'The silly bugger clobbered the horse trough.' He took a sniggering breath, 'The bloody horse trough. Whang! Straight through the flowers and into the bloody horse trough. Silly bugger.' He slid down the side of the ute until he was sitting in the mud, giggling.

She wrapped the dressing gown tighter around herself and strode into the rain. The yard was inches deep and she was instantly drenched.

Pozzer looked up with a stupid, unfocused grin.

She bent down until they were almost nose to nose. She could smell the stink of stale beer, the rankness of rotten teeth. 'Get the hell out of here,' she screamed. 'Go on. Just piss off. You scungy little maggot.'

He tried to turn away but she wasn't having it. She yanked his face back around. Even in the soaking rain his hair felt greasy.

'You heard me. Get lost. Now, piss off.'

'Jeezus,' he bubbled. Not grinning now. And again, 'Jeezus.'

'Just piss off.'

He scrambled across the yard on hands and knees while she kept on screaming and sobbing. 'Piss off, piss off, piss off.'

He finally gained his feet and staggered off down the drive. 'Jeezus, Jeezus.' Into the dark, into the rain.

The rain was solid. She was soaked and she could feel it filling her boots. The dressing gown stuck to her like a second skin. Now there was lightning and the hammering of thunder right overhead. She looked around, disorientated by the rain streaming down her face and the strobing flashes of lightning. For a moment, she couldn't find her useless husband.

She didn't remember picking up the old spade. It was just there, in her hands and swinging in a wide arc as he emerged from behind their ute. He held his arms out straight from his sides, hands turned forward in a vague gesture of 'What's going on?' He might have actually said it. If he did, the words were carried away by the storm. Besides, she was past hearing him.

It was a glancing blow. Enough for him, in his drunken idiocy, to stagger sideways and take one lurch head-first into the edge of their ute's open door. She heard the crack of breaking bone even above the crack of lightning. He dropped like a bullock in a slaughterhouse, into the mud.

It was hard yakka, it took until near-dawn, but she got the hole dug. Between the peppercorn and the shed. There were quite a lot of roots but she chopped them through with the old axe and kept on digging until she judged it to be deep enough. The lightning helped; she didn't need to risk a lantern. And then the storm blew itself out and a full moon shone through the scudding, fracturing clouds.

It was a good hole, a hole to be proud of. In other circumstances, she might have been well pleased to show it off. There was nearly a foot of water in the bottom, so he made quite a splash when she rolled him in. Then she filled it in and backed the ute over it. The last time anyone would ever drive it.

As the first milky light brought on the arguments of magpies and kookaburras, she lifted the bonnet and smashed the distributor cap with a brick. Then she bent methodically from wheel to wheel and let the air out of each of the tyres.

Once inside, she dried herself off and put on clothes and make-up. Then she got the boys' breakfast and walked them to school before heading on to the bakery.

It was an ordinary morning, the air crisp and clear after last night's downpour. People dodged puddles as they went about their usual routines. She felt a bit tired but otherwise ordinary…normal.

Lachlan James came into the shop at ten o'clock. He stood back, cap under his arm, as she finished serving old Mrs Waverley. A sausage roll and a Banbury slice.

As the brassy little doorbell tinkled Mrs Waverley's departure, he stepped forward. 'Good morning,' he said. All very formal. 'I wonder if you could tell me where I might find your husband.'

She shrugged. This was all expected. 'Lazy bugger's probably sleeping it off somewhere. He wasn't in the bed when I left this morning. Could be asleep in the ute. I didn't look this morning.'

'Well, no,' said the policeman. 'I've already been around to your place. And I checked your ute. He wasn't in there.'

'Then I wouldn't have a clue. Anyway, what do you want him for? What's the useless so-and-so been up to?'

'Well...' This was getting awkward. 'Apparently he crashed into the horse trough last night. Made a right mess of it. You must have seen the damage to the ute.'

'What damage?' She was doing well at this. 'To our ute? Christ, I never saw the ute this morning. We left out the front. How bad is it?'

'Do you mean the ute or the horse trough?'

'The ute. No, the horse trough. No...well, I mean, both of them.' She really was doing well at this, should be in the movies.

Constable James shuffled on the spot. 'Well, your ute's a real mess. Looks like a bent tie-rod and a lot of damage to the front suspension. The front is all stoved in and it looks like all the tyres are ruptured. Never seen that before. He must have hit the kerb with a right wallop to bugger all the tyres.'

She shook her head in what she hoped looked like disbelief. 'Christ, What about the trough?'

There was only one horse trough in town. It was the memorial to those lost in the Great War. A big slab of hollowed granite with a brass plaque. She'd never seen a horse in the main street, let alone a horse drinking from the memorial horse trough. Alongside the trough was a recently erected plinth for a Second World War memorial. The council had done a pretty good job with a flower bed and a couple of benches. People often took their pies there when the weather was good.

'The trough's been knocked off its base but it seems to be intact. Most of the damage has been done to the flower beds. One of the benches is firewood.' He hesitated. 'I have to tell you that a lot of people are pretty pissed off with your bloke. It's like a kind of desecration.'

This was a good time to change direction. She added a tremor to her voice and raised it in anger. The tremor was phoney but the anger was real. 'For starters, he's not "my bloke". He hasn't been "my bloke" since, since I found out what a bloody bullshit artist he was. He's been hitting the booze every night and I've given up trying to keep track of him. I didn't know anything about an accident last night until you told me just then. I'm not surprised. He's been an accident looking for somewhere to happen.'

She was about to go on when Dave from the stock agency came breezing in for his morning custard tart. He was closely followed by Maisie from the pub for the daily order of three loaves.

Lachlan played it like a real gent. He nodded to her, put on his cap. 'Right then,' he said. 'I'll be off. See you later.'

She left the window half open and climbed back into bed. It was cool enough to warrant a blanket and it felt good, somehow secure.

The sound, this time caught in wakefulness. From inside the house, a tiny, sharp click.

'Who's there?' Not a timid question, an angry demand. Who dares bring even the slightest flicker of fear to this, my own home?

Louder. 'What is it?' The single blanket pulled back, one foot seeking the floor, ready to pounce, to protect.

'It's just me, Mum. I needed a drink'

Sagging back onto the tepid mattress. All anger instantly gone. He just needed a drink. A satisfactory confirmation that a mother's instincts remain ingrained and ready for action.

She moves to the window and lets the freshening breeze wash over her. She looks beyond the yard, beyond their ute and their back fence to the mallee.

On a warm summer's night, with a gentle breeze washing the moonlight from uncountable silver leaves, the mallee can be enchanting.

Might go for a walk out there tomorrow. It's been a while.

She hears him padding back down the passage and then climbing back into his bed. It feels like tomorrow will be a warm one.

The Popular Copper

Curlew, the Riverland, 1958

Sergeant Peter Diamond wound down the driver's window and reached over to the back seat for his metal Thermos.

He could just as easily sneak back to the police station for his morning brew or simply walk through the adjoining door into the station house kitchen and share a cuppa with his wife. Unlikely; she'd probably be off at some club, or group, or flock of some sort. The Curlew Garden Club, or the United Flower Arrangers Guild, or the Curlew Hospital Volunteers, or the Curlew Ladies Bridge Club. For someone who bellyached endlessly when he was transferred to the Riverland, she seemed to be finding plenty of distractions.

This was his favourite spot, the lookout. Sitting in his new FC Holden police car on the high ground from where he could look down on Curlew – his domain.

It was a good view. Not particularly high as lookouts go, but a good place for tourists to take a photo. There was even room for them to turn their caravans round because the lookout also doubled as the car park for Saint Margaret's Church. Mind you, if you towed a caravan up here on a Sunday, you might find yourself waiting for the church service to finish before the congregation wandered back to their cars and left enough space for you to turn round. It was not uncommon for tourists to find themselves stuck up here with no option but to enjoy the view for an hour and a half.

Curlew had grown into a substantial and prosperous river town since it started life as not much more than a riverboat stop. From his vantage point, the sergeant could just make out the original old wharf where the paddle-steamers once took on firewood for their boilers and wool bales for their customers.

The back blocks still produced a lot of wool and grain but these days anyone within cooee of the Murray was growing fruit. Networks of channels now carried the precious water to vast groves of citrus and stone fruits growing on both sides of the river. Trucks now carried big wooden crates of oranges and big bins of apricots from the Curlew blockers to the juicing and canning factories in Renmark.

Dried apricots fetched the best money, so most of the locals picked up a few extra quid by cutting and stoning the fruit in the blockers' sheds at night. The wooden trays of halved apricots were stacked under white canvas tarpaulins to be soused in sulphur fumes overnight and then laid out on drying racks, just chicken-wire shelves stretched between wooden frames, to be desiccated by the sun.

The cutting sheds became the town's social centres during the summer. Peter Diamond's wife, Dianne, often worked an evening shift in one of the sheds. They didn't really need the threepence per tray but she enjoyed the company and often picked up a few titbits of local gossip. Dianne Diamond thrived on gossip and sometimes, when she and her husband were on rare speaking terms, she inadvertently played the role as a copper's snitch.

The sergeant was known to be quite selective when it came to applying his version of the law. Diamond's penalties for law-breaking were adjusted according to where the miscreant stood on his ladder of acceptability. His criteria had been accepted by the majority of Curlew's good citizens who, while not agreeing with all of his personal prejudices and protocols, took a certain comfort in his consistency. You knew where you stood with Peter Diamond even if, on occasion, you found yourself standing in something unpleasant. Besides, you had a choice; you could either challenge the burly representative of the law or you could turn a blind eye to his methods. The good folk of Curlew put their telescopes to their blind eyes and, like the first monkey, saw no evil.

Out-of-towners stood on a lower rung and so usually felt the long and muscular arm of Diamond's law. An unrecognised vehicle, incorrectly parked, would attract a roadworthiness check guaranteed to reveal enough faults to bankrupt the owner. By way of contrast, an approved local could park his car on the sergeant's foot and receive nothing more than a suggestion to be more careful in future.

Members of the RSL were similarly beyond reproach. Peter Diamond had served with distinction in the Pacific arena and was contemptible of anyone who had avoided military service. Many of the smaller farms that surrounded Curlew were worked by soldier-settlers and all of them enjoyed the sergeant's top-rung immunities. On the other hand, those who had avoided military service need only sneeze to find themselves charged with causing a disturbance.

A miscreant's age could also be a factor. First World War veterans could, should the mood take them, run naked and unrestrained through the streets with a loaded flame thrower whereas an eighteen-year-old spotty youth might receive a clip behind the ear for being nothing more than an eighteen-year-old spotty youth.

Paperwork was anathema to the sergeant, who believed that justice should be immediate and memorable. Very few minor wrongdoers received written statements because such niceties took time to write and were, therefore, not immediate. A clip behind the ear, a kick up the bum or a thorough thumping were all immediate and memorable and could be tailored to suit the offence. This is where the sergeant's training in unarmed close combat, so effective in the tropical jungles of Asia, came to the fore. An abusive and violent drunk might find himself, suddenly and unexpectedly, in such crippling agony that he wouldn't be able to walk, or eat, or scratch himself for a week. There wouldn't be a mark on him, but he would remember who didn't put it there. It was immediate and it was memorable. Second-time offenders weren't offered the luxury of a good thumping; they were booked. And, because the sergeant hated paperwork, he made it worth his while. When Sergeant Diamond put pen to paper a simple drunk-and-disorderly could rapidly come a violent-criminal-assault-with-intent-to-cause-grievous-bodily-harm-and-threaten-life.

It was through pure good fortune that Sergeant Diamond's reputation was complemented by a popular radio series called *Dick Diamond: Private Detective*, which was written by Blake Edwards and starred the popular Dick Powell. Very few Curlew radios weren't tuned into *Dick Diamond: Private Detective* on Monday nights, and much of Tuesday morning's chinwag revolved around the latest crime-smashing exploits of the Daring Dick. Dick Diamond was immensely popular.

The real-life Peter Diamond shared little in common with the crusty and cliché-driven radio detective but it was not uncommon for a muddled Curlew citizen to congratulate him on arresting the latest gangland boss. He always accepted the praise on the grounds that, firstly, it would cause embarrassment were he to point out that the gangland boss lived in Chicago rather than Curlew and, secondly, and in a roundabout way, these little flashes of mistaken identity enhanced his popularity. And Sergeant Peter Diamond had an insatiable hunger, a necessity, for the admiration of others. This also explained why he rarely corrected anyone who chose to call him Dick Diamond instead of Sergeant Diamond, unless they were trying to be sarcastic, in which case they received something immediate and memorable.

One of the frustrations of coppering is knowing that someone is a crook but not being able to pin it on him. Sergeant Peter Diamond had overcome this exasperation by inventing crimes that could be pinned onto those whom he knew to be criminals. To catch a known thief, all you have to do is nick something yourself, chuck the stolen item over the thief's fence during the night and then discover it, in his possession, next morning. Case closed, thief behind bars. The sergeant had no qualms about stretching his side of the law if it meant collaring someone on the other side. His unique slant on the means to an end argument had seen him develop a bag full of tailor-made crimes ready to be pinned on any uncooperative criminals.

Women and girls were, in the sergeant's eyes, incapable of

misdemeanour. Foolishness, certainly. Irrationality, of course. But wanton criminal behaviour, unlikely. The fairer sex perched high on his biased ladder of acceptability. One or two of them fluttered just above it.

Not so for those unfortunate enough to have been born an Aboriginal or an Asian or, for that matter, anyone speaking with an accent. Peter Diamond's prejudices were unshakeable, his bigotry was relentless, his prejudgements unbending.

It would probably be true to say that, to a greater or lesser degree, a lot of Curlew shared his racist views, his intolerances, his chauvinisms. The difference was that most of Curlew – the farmers, the shopkeepers, the housewives and the schoolkids – could navigate their way through their days without needing to confront their prejudices. They could avoid people who were different. They could sidestep the issues and, by doing so, pretend that they weren't really bigots and that Curlew was free of discrimination. The sergeant, with his immediate and memorable approach to country-town law enforcement, shielded the good townsfolk from having to confront distasteful issues. They approved with a wink and a nod. Such methods might not hold water in a court of law but you got what you deserved and that was the end of the matter. Besides, Peter Diamond was a popular bloke. And it didn't pay to question a popular bloke because he was…well, popular.

So Sergeant Peter Diamond enjoyed all of the benefits that come from being a popular country town cop. People waved to him as he cruised by on his three-times-a-day laps of the town. He was expected to attend community functions both officially, as a representative of law and order, and unofficially, because he was a popular bloke. And he enjoyed being a popular bloke. In fact, the sergeant practised a sort of aggressively competitive popularity. The idea of anyone else enjoying equal or, heaven forbid, greater popularity, was not to be entertained.

He always pitched in at school sports days, Christmas parades, fund-raisers and working bees. Drinkers didn't slink away when he strolled into the front bar of the Lady Augusta Hotel and he always stood for his shout when he was off duty. He never accepted a freebie, always paid for his haircuts and insisted that the two junior constables who made up the Curlew Police Force did the same.

Life was good, crime rates were acceptable, or, rather, the rates of reported crimes were acceptable. He was popular. Everyone liked Peter Diamond and Peter Diamond liked everybody…almost. His wife didn't like him very much and there were two blokes who really gave him the shits.

One of them lived in the manse not more than fifty yards from where he now sat. The Reverend Douglas Trembarth, the pastor of Saint Margaret's Church, the church that shared the car park with the lookout. Churches always commandeered the high ground.

There were two things – no, three things – about Trembarth that really ruffled Diamond's feathers. Firstly, he was a Pom. The sergeant's wide-ranging prejudices included Poms. True, most of them were of an acceptable colour and most Australians came from Pommy stock but Peter Diamond, ex-soldier, held very strong views about some of the bloody stupid things that the Poms had done during the war. Stupid things that had cost Aussie lives. And, come to think of it, not just the most recent war; a lot of Aussies had lost their lives in the first war because of Pommy stupidity.

He'd heard that Trembarth hadn't joined the Pommy army, that he was a bloody dodger. Not that Peter Diamond had any great respect for Pommy soldiers, but he had even less respect for blokes who didn't join up.

London, 20 September 1940

The Reverend Douglas Trembarth didn't need to check the woman's pulse because he could see that she was breathing. She would be first live one that they'd rescued this night.

He called back to Trev who was waiting at the top of the ladder. 'She's all right, Trev. Looks like her legs are twisted under the mattress. I'll pull the bed back a bit and see if I can shift it.'

'Good-oh,' answered his offsider. 'How's the floor feel?'

He stayed at the top of the ladder. First rule when you're faced with a risky rescue situation: only one man to venture into the dangerous places until they'd been made safe. It was usually Reverend Douglas who fronted up to the dicey business. Trev was happy for Doug to risk his neck, this was the fifth hellishly dangerous place they'd attended. Besides, Doug was a bantamweight; a little fella, all muscles and sinews. He could squeeze through narrow gaps like a ferret chasing rabbits and he didn't weigh enough to cause collapses. Trev, by contrast, was a bit...well, cuddly. Not really built for rescue work. Not really built for anything much...except cuddling.

'Floor's a bit wobbly,' answered Douglas.

There was an ominous splintering sound and the whole building shuddered as if to confirm his appraisal.

The woman gave a little whimper as he shifted the bed and pulled the heavy old flock mattress away from her legs. She was a small lady in her fifties, dressed for bed but now embarrassingly dishevelled and covered in dust. It took a moment for Douglas to recognise her.

'Here, it's Mrs Watkins, isn't it? Do you remember me, Mrs Watkins? It's Douglas Trembarth. I used to live two streets over. My dad's still living there – Maurice, Maurice Trembarth.'

She twisted to look into his eyes but there was no hint of recognition. She tried to speak but all she managed was a gasping cough.

'No wonder,' he thought. 'The poor duck has just been blown out of her bed and her house is a ruin.'

There were no obvious signs of injury. He very gently ran his hands around her ankles and arms. Then he rearranged her bedclothes to preserve her modesty. Not that it really mattered; she was bewildered beyond modesty.

'Hang on, luv,' he said. 'We'll soon have you away from here. Can you move your feet?'

'You might need to get shifting, Douglas,' called Trev from the void that had, until recently, been a wall. 'This floor's about to give way, and there's smoke coming from down the street. Let's get the lady down the ladder and away from here.'

'Righto. Come on, luv. Don't try to stand up. We'll crawl over to Trev and he'll give us a hand.'

Her disorientation helped. She followed their instructions obediently so that even the risky manoeuvre of getting her onto the ladder went without a hitch. She was too confused to feel fear.

The smoke was thickening and they could hear the sharp crackling of fire not far off. An old fire tender, a museum piece, jangled past. The tinny and irregular bell was quickly lost against the background bedlam as it disappeared into the haze. It was followed by an old Morris van sporting a roughly painted red cross that didn't disguise the fact that it had been seconded from J. Simpson, Grocer and Hardware. Trev waved it down.

They laid Mrs Watkins on the only patch of pathway that wasn't littered with rubble and then Douglas turned back to the devastated house.

'Wait here, Trev. I won't be a tick.'

'Hang on there, Douglas. Where're you going? You're not going inside? It's ready to collapse, mate.'

'It'll hold. I'll just be a minute.' He climbed back up the ladder and disappeared into the bedroom.

There was a warning groan of stressed timber and a cascade of roof tiles shattered on the rubble sending shards of ceramic into the street. The unsupported floor sagged further and things, personal bedroom things, began to tumble out. A brass alarm clock gave a terminal clang as it hit the path. It was followed by a single slipper that clipped one of the ambulance orderlies as they eased Mrs Watkins onto a stretcher. He swore.

Douglas reappeared at the ladder and threw down two bulging pillow cases. Then he grabbed a third and shimmied down the ladder. 'Get moving, Trev. Grab the ladder,' he called as he gathered up the pillow cases. 'It's coming down.'

The orderlies were gently manoeuvring their patient into J. Simpson's van.

Douglas added the pillowcases. 'You chaps make sure these things stay with Mrs Watkins,' he instructed. 'When you get her to hospital, make sure the nurses know that these things belong to her. Hang on...' He retrieved one of the cases and pulled out a handbag. After quickly rummaging through it, he extracted a lipstick and wrote, in huge red letters, 'Watkins' on all three pillow cases. 'There,' he said. 'But you fellows still check that they stay with her.'

'Blimey, mate,' questioned the driver. 'What's in 'em, the family fortune?'

'No. Her dressing gown and some clothes and smalls. That one's got her handbag and all the bits and pieces from her dressing table. This one's got two photo albums and a lot of framed photos from her room...' He paused and then sagged to sit on the kerb. This was his fifteenth straight night on duty. He'd pulled dozens of bodies from the rubble of bombed homes and rescued a few that might have otherwise perished. He was exhausted. Looking up at the driver he croaked, 'Her house is going to fall down and probably burn before the night's out. Her husband's away in the merchant marines and her son is somewhere in France. She'll be needing this stuff.'

The driver patted him on the shoulder. 'We'll look after her, mate.' He closed the rear door of the van. 'How do you know so much about her? Did you live around here?'

Douglas waved his hand vaguely in the direction from which they'd arrived. 'Yes, in Cremourne Street. It's two streets over.'

The orderlies glanced at each other. 'Not any more, mate,' said the driver. 'We passed Cremourne Street on our way here. It's been well and truly clobbered. Hardly a house left standing.'

Douglas sat transfixed. The implications of this news took a moment to explode into his exhausted brain. His father still lived in Cremourne Street. He rose to his feet awkwardly and took a few lurching steps into the street. And then he was sprinting, wildly, arms thrashing at the reddening haze.

'Ahhhh, hell,' groaned Trev. And then, as he ran after him, 'Hang on, Douglas. Wait up, mate.'

A police car, windows ruddy with fiery reflections, angled across the entrance to Cremourne Street. An overweight bobby leaned against the bonnet, indifferent to the destruction behind him. When he saw Douglas approaching at speed, he pushed himself away from the vehicle and held up a hand. He managed, 'Sorry, sir, but I can't let –' before Douglas cannoned into him and sent him sprawling.

It took Douglas a little while to identify where his father's house, his family home, had stood. Oddly, it was the old wooden shed that he recognised. It was one of just a handful of structures that, by pure chance, hadn't been razed. It leant at a precarious angle against the one remaining wall of the neighbour's house and, through the sagging doors, he could just make out his father's pride and joy: the 1935 Wolseley Hornet.

Trev found Douglas staring blankly at the destruction that had been the focus of his boyhood. He put his hand on the young priest's shoulder. 'Doug, I'm sorry. I spoke to the rescue chaps. Your dad, they couldn't find him. It looks like he didn't make it.'

Douglas turned to his mate. Tears, mixed with the dust of his night's work, painted a face of pure despair. 'No, I shouldn't think anyone could have.'

He groped for the remnants of a low brick garden wall. Trev took his arm and eased him down until he was sitting awkwardly. It was remarkably quiet; the rescue teams had left, nothing left to save here. Distant sirens were muffled by the shrouding smoke.

'He should have come and stayed with us, Trev. Evelyn and me. We begged him, begged him. But he wanted to stay here, where he and Mum raised me. Where all of his…his…life was, '

His voice was drowned out by the noisy return of the old fire engine. It was obviously no match for whatever was burning down the road and seemed to be just careering around with no definite purpose. They watched it disappear. It took Trev a little while to register that its tinny jangling bell had been replaced by a persistent and rasping sound from behind them.

'What's that?'

Douglas was sitting with head in hands. 'What?'

'That noise, like a horn.'

'Fire engine.'

'No, more like a car horn. Sounds like the battery's nearly dead.' He stood up. 'Listen, mate, we ought to shift. There's nothing to be done here. Why don't we try the hospital, and the Red Cross station? They might know something. Hang on, there it is again.' He swung round. 'Sounds like it's coming from that shed.'

Douglas was on his feet. 'Shit, the Wolseley, C'mon.'

The Wolseley Hornet had been the first new car that the Trembarths had ever owned. Douglas had gone with his mum and dad to pick it up and they'd used up the best part of a tank full of petrol taking the long way home, a really long way home. It was a beautiful thing to drive, six cylinder, overhead cam and good brakes.

Douglas had learned to drive in the Hornet. It had taken the family on wonderful motoring holidays to Scotland and Wales. It took them to church every Sunday even though the church was less than half a mile away.

One terrible day, they'd rushed Mum to hospital in the Hornet when she collapsed suddenly. A week later, it carried them to her funeral.

Douglas had courted Evelyn in the Hornet. Nothing untoward; the Hornet had standards. Last year, it had taken Douglas to the church to marry Evelyn.

The first thing that the senior Mr Trembarth said when they reached the shed was, ''Bout time you buggers got here. Been blasting the horn for the past hour. Battery's near flat.'

'Sorry, Dad,' choked Douglas. It was hard to speak through the sobs and the smiles. 'Been a bit tied up with rescues and suchlike. Can you get out?'

His father was sitting behind the wheel of the Wolseley. The back seat was covered in boxes and cases, keepsake stuff that he'd thought needed saving.

'Well, I could. Wouldn't be much point 'cause the shed doors are stuck. I've been here since the bombing started, safer here than in the house.'

'The house is gone, Dad.'

'Yer, thought so. Helluva bang. That's when the shed took on a lean and the doors got stuck halfway.'

Trev was wrestling with the wooden doors. He called to his mate. 'If we swing this door back far enough, it would probably act like a brace for long enough to squeeze the car out, Doug. How's your dad? Could he steer it while we push?'

'I'm fine,' answered the senior Trembarth. 'You young buggers put your shoulders to it and I'll steer her out.'

Curlew, the Riverland, 1958

Sergeant Diamond poured the last of the tea into the metal cup, knocked it back in a single gulp and screwed the cup back onto the top of the Thermos. He glanced at the church and the manse across the car park and scowled. The Reverend Douglas Trembarth was out on the front lawn polishing his bloody Wolseley. His father was sitting in a rocker on the veranda. He was a little bugger, the reverend, built like a bloody bantam. Behaved like one too, kind of clucky and fussy.

They doted on that car, the Wolseley, always polishing it. Then chuffing around town with the old bloke in the back seat like bloody royalty. Waving to everyone, and everyone waving back. The Reverend Trembarth and his family were popular around Curlew; this was another thing that annoyed Peter Diamond.

Apparently the Trembarths had emigrated to Australia straight after the war, something about the wife needing a dry climate because she'd got some sort of breathing problem. The old bloke, the reverend's father, had come with them and they'd also brought that bloody stupid 1935 Wolseley. Must have cost a bloody fortune to get it here. Why would you bother? They could have bought a decent Aussie car with what it cost to bring that bloody pile of junk all the way from Pommyland.

Another annoying thing was that Dianne Diamond; the copper's wife, had befriended Evelyn Trembarth, the vicar's wife. They did churchy things together, visiting hospital patients, sewing bees, trading tables and church fetes. Dianne had never seen the inside of a church before they married. Now she spent half her time mixing with the Bible-bashers.

Something else that really made the copper's blood boil was that the reverend had twice complained about his immediate and memorable methods. Diamond had received reminders from the police discipline board about correct procedure. Nothing admonishing, just reminders. But enough reminders could add up to a reprimand.

It was all because of those Cogginses, that weird bunch down by the river. They were as thick as thieves; the Cogginses and the Trembarths. No understanding why; maybe because both blokes had dodged the army. Otherwise they were like cheese and chalk. The Trembarths were Poms, right down to their bloody stupid Pommy car. The Cogginses were a bunch of mixed-breed darkies. Well, mostly. The husband, Roland, was a white bloke. Married an Abo woman from Darwin and lived with her and her sister and a bloody tribe of young 'uns from heaven knows where.

The sergeant didn't like Aborigines. He liked white blokes who married Aborigines even less. And white blokes who married Aborigines and didn't fight in the war, they were the lowest form of life.

Darwin, 19 February 1942

Father Roland Coggins sat on the veranda sipping a sweet black tea and pondering his crisis. Or, truth be known, his crises. He had a few of them.

His leg was giving him gyp today so he'd been forced to use the cane walking stick now propped alongside his seat. The pain and awkwardness, legacies of a double bout of childhood polio and scarlet fever, hadn't bothered him much lately; he'd always walk with a limp but, hopefully, not always with the stick. Otherwise he was as fit as a mallee bull; tall and good-looking in a way that seemed to attract glances from the ladies. Someone had once likened him to Errol Flynn – probably not a suitable comparison for a priest.

He stretched his leg. This was one of his bad days; they always somehow made him feel edgy, somehow foreboding, like a portent.

Mind you, everyone was feeling edgy these days. Singapore had fallen just a few days ago and there didn't seem to any stopping the bloody Japs. Rumours of invasion were rife; every day brought panicked stories of landing craft entering the harbour. Even the coast watch were mistaking fishing boats for battleships. People had been packing up and leaving Darwin for weeks.

The disability – God how he hated the term – had marked him as unfit for military duties. He'd tried to enlist but only because every else had joined up. The knock-back had been a bit humiliating, although, truth be known, he couldn't see himself in khaki.

He'd found a satisfactory compromise through the army chaplain, who was a decent chap but a bit overwhelmed. He was of Protestant persuasion and welcomed Roland as an unofficial Roman Catholic assistant, one of many civilians whom the army commander viewed through a pragmatically blind eye. So the young priest split his time between the base camp and the orphanage.

Sometimes, though, even on good days, he carried the stick by way of explaining why he was one of the few young men not engaged in the conflict, the conflict that had nearly destroyed Europe and was now doing the same to the Pacific. The stick legitimised him; no one questioned the courage of a bloke with a limp and a stick.

From behind him came kitchen noises, intermittent chatter accompanied by the clatter of tinware. Short snatches of song and brief giggles were muted. The orphanage discouraged things loud or lively.

Well, not the orphanage as such. It was the two nuns who ran the place: Sister Ruth and Sister Beatrice. They were, along with his crook leg, on Roland's list of why his life was maggoty. In his weekly letter to his father back in the Riverland, he called them 'Satan's penguins', always in their black habits and always crotchety.

They were both large women, dominating figures who loomed over their young charges like storm clouds full of thunder and threat. Sister Ruth was never without a scowl and Sister Beatrice was never without a riding crop, a nasty little black leather switch which she constantly tapped against her own flank. It was an affectation that always put Roland in mind of a military officer tapping his swagger stick against his boots. He had never seen her actually hit a child but the implied threat would be obvious even to the youngest.

The children, all thirty-six of them aged somewhere between five and eleven, lived in a state of constant and nervous wariness. The sisters enforced their rules mercilessly. And their rules were many: no running, no shouting, no laughing – no behaving like children.

So the orphanage was high on Roland's list of depressing things. Well, it wasn't only the orphanage, although God knew it was a wretched place. No, he was depressed by all of Darwin; he hated it. As a first posting for a newly ordained priest, it was as close to hell as the devil's doormat. Hot, humid, insect-infested and sinful to the point where inventing the most odious crimes was a competitive sport; they probably presented trophies.

Another brief snatch of song from the kitchen caught the young priest in mid-lament for the single most salient cause of his inner turmoil: Marie.

Marie Hannan was the younger of two sisters, real birth-sisters, not like those two hooded horrors with the cowls and the scowls and the crops that called themselves sisters. Marie and Millie were two young part-Aboriginal women who worked as domestics for the orphanage and shared a small cottage behind the kitchen. There was little, other than their dark complexions and sunny personalities, to suggest that they were, in fact, sisters. Millie, the elder of the two, was short and quite dumpy, while Marie was taller and willowy, albeit a somewhat curvaceous willow.

At eighteen, Marie was the most alluring creature that Roland had ever seen. Somewhere amongst Marie's forebears lurked the most beautiful of Aboriginal, Asian and Caucasian ancestors and each had contributed to an elegance that would have had Rossetti weeping into his palette.

Roland spent a lot of time thinking about Marie.

A chanted drone from one of the weatherboard classrooms brought the priest back to his gritty reality. Sister Ruth was drilling her class in the repetition of tables. Probably a parroting of pounds and ounces, or perhaps of pounds and shillings. No doubt useful stuff, useful knowledge that would help the children when they left the orphanage for a life of inevitable menial servitude. Not much point in filling their little coloured heads with useless poetry or history or literature. Basic cookery, and sewing, and laundry was all that the girls would need. Basic practical crafts for the boys. Basic reading and simple maths for all. Useful stuff, quite enough for anyone with the horizon of a lizard.

The sisters must have recited the same tables in the same droning tones to a hundred blank faces for a hundred blank years. Theirs was an existence of repetition, of never-varying routines, of never-questioned dogma, of never-softening bitterness.

Roland pondered the two pairs of sisters, one paired by birth, the other by doctrine. It was difficult to see how a single species could have given rise to such disparity. Where Sister Ruth scowled, sister Marie smiled. While Sister Beatrice carried a crop, sister Millie carried a song.

The children loved the real sisters. Roland loved Marie.

His love was his melancholy. Roman Catholic priests weren't allowed to love women other than in the approved spiritual sense. Roland was sure that he did love Marie in the approved spiritual sense. But he was equally sure that he also loved her in the disapproved sense. He was getting perilously close to at least one of the seven deadly sins.

He'd been invited to dine with the army chaplain several times. The young Protestant churchman lived with his wife and two toddlers in a tidy little off-base house. They seemed singularly happy and no less devout for turning their backs, and obviously their other bits, on celibacy. Same God, different canon. Roland added Envy to his list of Broken Sins.

Sometimes, usually at night as he sweated and swatted on his canvas camp bed, Roland even considered quitting the ministry. Not so much through a crisis of faith but more through a growing sense that the manifestation of religion, the church, with all of its politics, its hierarchies, its demarcations and its many unhinged acolytes, didn't accommodate Roland's simple faith. It certainly didn't accommodate Roland's infatuation with a beautiful, mixed-race young lady.

He was fairly certain that Marie was interested in him. It was her suggestion that the children found him intimidating because he wore the traditional black, the same black that they associated with the sisters, the nuns. When he reverted to wearing lighter street clothes, he immediately found it easier to get along with the youngsters.

It was Marie who suggested that he help out with the cooking classes, the only classes that the nuns allowed Millie and Marie to teach, and the only classes that the children enjoyed. They made scones, they burnt sausages and they stirred enormous vats of chutney, Millie's speciality, made from whatever fruit and vegetables were in seasonal abundance.

It was Marie who, when the children had reluctantly left the kitchen tables to chant the times tables, joined Roland at the sink to scrub the dishes and accidentally touch hands beneath the suds.

The young priest swished the tea dregs into the dust of the quadrangle and, with the aid of his stick, unfolded his lanky frame to the vertical. He checked his watch: a quarter to ten. Still a couple of hours till lunch. He should be all right to scrounge another cuppa before helping with the lunch preparations. He did a quick count back through Millie's ten-day lunch cycle. Yes, today would be cheese and chutney sandwiches with a slice of melon and an iced oatmeal biscuit sprinkled with coconut.

And then the first bomb hit the harbour and the air was suddenly full of sirens and aircraft and explosions, and screams.

They'd had an evacuation plan of sorts. Roland had routinely checked their two vehicles, a rather battered Morris ex-school bus and an even rougher Morris light truck with a canvas-covered tray. The fuel tanks were full and he'd strapped two extra four-gallon tins to each tow-bar. The batteries were charged and he'd secured a dozen old cameleers' water canisters under the seats of each vehicle.

Sister Beatrice's rather vague plan was for everyone to crowd into the bus and she'd drive them south and to safety. Roland was to gather useful stuff into the truck and follow the bus. She hadn't defined what she meant by useful stuff nor calculated the improbability of packing four adults and thirty-six children into a twenty-four-seat bus.

Her idea of safety was also somewhat fuzzy and seemed to be fixed on the illusion that a mission school at Katherine would provide sanctuary. Roland tried to explain that an overladen bus would probably average about forty miles per hour and carry enough fuel for about three hundred miles. An invading Japanese army wouldn't have much trouble catching up and was unlikely to be halted by a mission school at Katherine.

The underlying problem was that a Japanese invasion didn't fit with the nuns' unbending routines and unending repetitions. Change was anathema, change was beyond their wit.

Roland had pondered on some variations to Sister Beatrice's plans. So had Millie and Marie.

Only one bomb came close. Close enough to rip the roof from the sisters' cottage and shower the entire orphanage with rocks and dirt. Close enough to shatter windows and knock everyone to the ground.

The cottage had deflected most of the blast away from the kitchen, so Marie and Millie were quickest to recover and swing their own plans into action. They had long since determined that they weren't going on the bus with the nuns.

Roland had been blown off the veranda but was quick to recover. He poked his head through the kitchen door just long enough to check that the women were all right. Then he made for the classrooms and, for the first time since he'd arrived at the orphanage, started throwing his weight around.

The little two-vehicle convoy, when it eventually drove away from the orphanage, wasn't as Sister Beatrice had vaguely envisioned it.

Roland led the way in the truck. On board with him were the kitchen sisters and seven children selectively plucked from the milling assemblage by Marie. The priest didn't understand her selection process; he couldn't tell what differentiated these seven from the rest. But she had obviously chosen with a purpose and her only muttered explanation was, 'These are my kids.' Millie had nodded knowingly and given Roland a look that said, 'Don't ask.' He didn't.

The rest of the children, reduced in number to twenty-five because four of the older boys had taken advantage of the confusion and shot through, were crammed into the bus with the nuns. Sister Beatrice had insisted on driving and was somewhat put out by having to follow Roland's truck rather than leading her flock out of danger. Roland suspected that, somewhere in the hullabaloo, Sister Beatrice had recast the Japanese as the Pharaoh's soldiers and herself as some sort of female Moses.

Every child carried at least one blanket and a paper bag containing what had been intended for lunch before the bombing. Every other scrap of tucker, down to the last mote of flour, had been loaded into the truck by Millie. It included no fewer than ninety-eight jars of her home-made chutney.

'Things,' grinned Millie. 'Could get fairly ripe in that bus.'

The sun was setting between lightning-strobed storm clouds as they arrived at Adelaide River. They were now part of a huge exodus from Darwin. Overloaded cars, trucks and motorbikes transformed the normally lonely Stuart Highway into a peak-hour crawl. Most of them continued into the dusk but Roland veered away from the highway and, with the bus following, headed towards a cluster of dim lights barely visible amongst trees.

Marie had claimed a place in the front seat. This would have been rather intoxicating for the young priest but for the small child that his heart's desire had wedged between them.

She raised her voice against the grinding-whine of the gearbox and spoke over the child's head. 'Where are we going?'

'Army depot,' he answered and slowed to a stop as two soldiers, rifles at the ready, flagged them down.

'Can you duck back to the bus and tell everyone to stay put?' he asked before climbing stiffly down from the cabin.

Marie watched as Roland was led away by one of the soldiers. The other, assured that the Japanese weren't invading by bus, leaned against a gatepost. She climbed down and walked to the bus.

Sister Ruth stuck her head out of a window and, in her shrillest squawk, demanded. 'What is it, Marie? Why have we stopped?'

'What does it look like?' snapped Marie. 'A flamin' funfair?' She advanced on the startled sister. It felt good to give the old bat a serve of her own vitriol. 'It's a bloody army depot,' she flung at the stunned nun. 'Roland's organising something. You're to keep everyone in the bus.' She was enjoying herself; bossing bullies is good sport.

She strode back to the truck, where she met Roland and three soldiers each carrying two square four-gallon petrol tins. Two of the tins went into the bus, the others into the back of the truck. Roland waved his thanks and climbed stiffly back into the cab. Carrying full petrol tins didn't help his crook leg.

Fat raindrops started to hammer on the roof and lightning dazzled the landscape. He was forced to raise his voice in answer to her raised eyebrow.

'They reckoned that they'll blow up all these depots if the Japs got close. Seemed like a waste of useful petrol, so I got a requisition note from the Darwin commander. This'll get us to Katherine with fuel to spare.'

Marie was quiet for a while. The raindrops had joined forces to become steady rain and the truck's single wiper did little but smear the windscreen.

'Are we going to stop at Katherine?' she asked.

'That seems to be Sister Beatrice's plan.'

'Yer, I know.' She looked over the intervening child. 'But, but what about us? Are we going to stop at Katherine?'

He shook his head. 'It's a stupid idea. If the Japs get into Darwin, they'll head down the Stuart as fast as they can. What's left of our army won't stop 'em. That's why they're planning on blowing up the fuel dumps.'

They drove on slowly. The rain was getting heavier.

'We'll have to pull over somewhere,' he shouted. 'I can't see a thing in this. Here, this'll do.'

They'd come to a gravelled area off to the side of the road. He led the bus into the cleared area and then stopped the engine.

Maria slid open the little rear window of the cab. 'Is everything all right back there, Millie?' she called.

'As well as can be expected,' answered her sister. 'The kids didn't mind being bounced around. My bum is numb. Are we stopping here?'

'At least until the rain stops,' explained Roland. 'Doesn't look like that'll happen for a while. See if you can grab a few winks while you can.'

Maria shut the window and turned to him. 'How far is it to Katherine?'

'About a hundred and thirty miles. Pine Creek's about seventy miles. We'll see if we can scrounge more petrol from the depot there.'

The younger sister pondered this for a while. 'Do we need more petrol? I thought that we'd have enough to get to Katherine.'

'We have, more than enough. I'm not planning on stopping in Katherine. If you and the nuns want to stop at the mission school, then so be it. One way or the other, I'm pushing on.'

There were sleepy snuffs from the child.

Maria lowered her voice to a whisper. 'But this truck belongs to the orphanage. We – you – can't just take it.'

Roland looked steadily at her. 'Then I'll be borrowing it. I'll return it when the Japs are pushed back. You said we. What –'

'Millie and me won't be stopping at Katherine with those two witches,' she hissed. 'We've had enough of them and their rotten ways. We'll come with you if you don't mind.'

Roland was surprised to wake up at daybreak. Surprised because he hadn't expected to fall asleep while sitting upright in the cabin of an old truck.

He looked across to where Maria was wedged between the door and the seat. Still asleep, she leaned forward as if to comfort the small child who had slumped across her lap, a beautiful Madonna beyond the best work of any Renaissance master, a tableau swathed in soft golden light. He slowly realised that the whole world was washed in gold. Even the tatty cabin of the truck had taken on an unlikely ethereal quality. He tore his gaze from Maria and to the spectacle beyond the windscreen.

His first impression was that of an enormous sea stretching forever. It took a moment for his slumber-numbed mind to register that it was fog – dense, gently billowing fog, lying waist-deep across the landscape so thickly that the ground was lost beneath it. The early sun, emerging from behind a screen of slender trees, lacquered the surface in shimmering gilt striated with deep purple shadows. Reflected under-light turned larger trees into theatrical backdrops growing from an unearthly, obfuscated stage.

Nothing moved but the quietly surging surface. Ocean-like, it lapped against the truck like the flood against the ark, so substantial, so defined, that it seemed to Roland that he could almost step from the truck's cabin and walk on it.

There was no sound, no breeze to riffle the leaves, no birds to chorus the dawn. Like the hushed respect demanded by great paintings in galleries, this was a miracle insisting on silence.

Roland had grown up on the Murray River, so he was familiar with floods. It was not unusual for the great watercourse to creep over its banks and inundate the river flats. They were usually benign events; rarely did they cause any real damage or inconvenience. Sometimes the floods were brief, only lasting for a week or two. Sometimes they might last for months. These were good times for young lads because the yabbies would proliferate and the set lines stretched across the shallows would snare great hauls of callop and cod.

Often, just on sunrise, the flooded plains would be shrouded by a thin mist. The panorama through the windscreen, albeit not a real flood, brought back memories of his youth, a time from before he took his religious orders, before they packed him off to Darwin.

He had already decided not to stop at Katherine but he hadn't really thought about a destination. His only concern had been to get the kids out of Darwin and beyond the Japanese bombing. But now, as he contemplated this wonderful sunrise, he knew that he was going back to the Riverland, to the Murray and the fruit block, his home.

He was brought back to the reality of the truck by a soft intake of breath. Maria was awake and gazing in wonder at the scene. Eventually she turned moist eyes to him and, careful not to disturb the sleeping child still recumbent on her lap, reached over and brushed his cheek with her fingertips. Then they just sat and watched.

Nothing could have more completely shattered that intimate moment. Nothing could have changed Roland's reverie to rage any quicker than the impatient horn blast from the old Morris bus.

Nothing could have been more unfitting than Sister Ruth's shrill 'Are you people awake? Father Coggins, are you awake?'

The very-much-awake father gripped the steering wheel with both hands and banged his head against it three times whilst uttering a short incantation. 'Shit, shit, shit.' Then, showing restraint worthy of a saint, he climbed down from the truck and approached Sister Ruth as she stood in the bus's bifold doorway. 'Yes, sister. We're all awake. Not much chance of anyone still being asleep now, is there?'

'Good,' replied the holy woman haughtily. 'We should be getting a move on, father. Perhaps you could tell Millie to prepare breakfast.'

Roland moved a step closer. Close enough for Sister Ruth to register that all was not to his liking. She retreated a step back into the bus.

'Nobody will be telling Millie anything, sister,' he hissed through clenched teeth. 'You might try asking but, in this instance, don't bother. As soon as this mist lifts enough to see the road, we'll be heading to Pine Creek for petrol. Perhaps you might try asking Millie about breakfast when we get there.'

He turned back to the truck but then paused in afterthought. 'Tell me, sister,' he asked in a deceptively mild tone, 'did you see the sunrise this morning?'

'Yes. Of course I did. I haven't slept a wink all night. Of course I saw the sun rise, along with this unpleasant fog. Why do you ask?'

'Unpleasant,' echoed the priest to himself. And then, in a voice that shook the parrots from their perches, 'You know, sister, praying for your soul would be a bloody waste of time. You haven't got one.'

Halfway back to the truck, he couldn't resist a final shot. 'God was here this morning, sister. He didn't show himself to you. Can't say that I blame him.'

The officer in charge of the Pine Creek depot was a boyish lieutenant who looked young enough to get into the cinema on a child's ticket. He helped to load another eight petrol tins into the truck and then asked the cook to organise a mountain of toast with plum jam. Milky tea was shared from army pannikins because they didn't have enough cups. Sister Ruth remained in the bus, wearing a face that could have peeled paint.

Over the impromptu breakfast, the officer shared the news that the Japs had bombed Darwin again just after Roland had led his small convoy out of the orphanage. Hundreds dead, dozens of ships sunk at anchor and all the fuel dumps in flames. Their evacuation had been timely.

To Roland's mind, the lieutenant was just a bit too excited about the attacks, a bit too eager. The sort of idealised zeal that drives rash young men to march mindlessly into enemy bayonets. And that wasn't all. To Roland's mind, the lieutenant was also a bit too interested in Maria, a bit too eager. He managed to sit next to her and personally serve her enough tea to float a boat and enough toast to pave a parade ground. He was panting like a puppy and came close to tripping over his own tongue. Roland was glad to get back on the road to Katherine, which he reckoned they should reach by early-afternoon.

He had spent an uncomfortable night in Katherine during his journey north to take up his appointment in Darwin. He had found it, like a frontier town in a bad Western, to be an ugly and noisy place. His first impression on his return was that it hadn't changed. Tim Holt could have played the Fargo Kid here, Gene Autry might have whistled the 'Gaucho Serenade'.

The mission school, a grim collection of timber-framed asbestos buildings surrounded by a high wire-mesh fence, was on the junction of Two Mile Creek and Katherine River.

Roland pulled over and climbed out of the truck to open the double gates. He waved the bus through, closed the gates, climbed back into the truck and started to drive away.

'Aren't we going in?' queried Marie as he accelerated away from the school.

'Why?' He replied. 'You didn't want to stay here, did you?'

'No, but I thought... No, well, shouldn't we say goodbye or something? Have you told the sisters that we're borrowing the truck? Have you told them where we're going?

Roland shifted down a gear and swung left onto the Stuart Highway. 'No, I haven't. I've told the sisters that staying in Katherine is a stupid idea. They didn't listen. There's nothing to stop the Japs bombing here after they've finished plastering Darwin.'

He had the truck up to speed, forty miles per hour. Faster than he'd been able with the bus in tow.

'The sisters won't have any use for the truck for a while. I'll bring it back after all the kerfuffle with the Japs is over. They won't have the resources to hold on in Australia for very long. The Yanks'll cut off their supply lines.'

He drove in silence for a while. 'Or I could just send them money to buy another truck. An old rattler like this couldn't be worth much.'

Maria stared at the road ahead. She had assumed that there'd be some sort of parting of the ways, something a bit dramatic. She'd even rehearsed a few choice farewell words for the sisters. Just driving away had been somehow disappointing, a bit of a let-down. But now, on reflection, she could see that not telling the sisters anything, just driving away and leaving them completely in the dark, was quite delicious. Leaving them in a state of confusion was a much more satisfactory reprisal than leaving them with a mere mouth full of insults.

She smiled across at the priest. 'Yer, sending money would be best. At least we wouldn't have to see those witches again. Have you decided where we're going? Is it Alice Springs?'

Her repeated use of 'we' was interesting. Did she mean just the two of them or did she include Millie and the kids in the back of the truck?

'I'm going a long way past the Alice,' he said. 'I'm thinking about going home, to the Riverland.'

'I don't anything about any River Land. How much further is it?'

He grinned. 'Not sure,' and, after a quick mental calculation, 'just a bit under two thousand miles, I reckon. Probably eight or ten days if this truck doesn't pack up.' He pondered some more as the miles ticked away and then, tentatively, 'Or I could take the train south from the Alice and you and the kids could keep the truck. You could go wherever you please.'

It was a blatantly provocative idea, not one that he wanted her to choose. She didn't answer. They drove on in silence for another mile.

'What do you think?' he probed.

'We'll see,' Maria replied coyly, and not believing for a moment that he'd leave her in Alice Springs. 'Where are we stopping tonight?'

He looked across at her. God, but she was beautiful. 'Mataranka's not far. There's a big pool of warm water. Bubbles up from underground. Kids can have a dip.'

'Me too,' she grinned.

He nearly drove into a ditch.

They parked the truck alongside a maze of cattle yards and an empty hay shed that could be most kindly described as picturesque. It was a basic structure of rough-cut poles struggling to support a sagging roof of rusted corrugated iron. At least the layer of old, remnant hay looked likely to provide a more comfortable sleeping place than the truck.

The thermal pool was reached by way of a path that meandered beyond the yards and through thickets of paper-barks and pandanus. There were signs that cattle sometimes came here but, apparently, not recently. The water was crystal-clear, deep and inviting.

'Tell yer what,' said Roland to Millie and Marie, 'why don't you ladies keep an eye on the kids and I'll go back and sort out the camp. I'll come down and have a dip when the kids have had enough.'

He was barely halfway back to the truck when the peace of the late afternoon gave way to the delighted shrieks and splashes that only happened when you mixed kids with water. It crossed his mind that Maria would be splashing around with them. It was a beguiling thought but his sometimes inconvenient sense of decency overcame the temptation to sneak back for a peep.

The day was nearly spent by the time everyone had enjoyed the pool and returned to camp. Millie fussed over the fire and knocked up a scratch meal based on her staples of sweet tea, damper and chutney.

The two sisters and the kids spread their blankets onto the old hay and made comfortable nests for themselves. There were a few hushed giggles but the excitement of the last two days had everyone feeling exhausted. Sleep came quickly.

Roland, determined to guard their petrol supplies, opted to sleep in the back of the truck. The night was warm, with just enough breeze to gently rattle the stiff pandanus leaves and to carry Darwin, the Japs and the nuns out of his thoughts.

Sometime after midnight he was wakened by Marie as she crept into his bed. She was gone before dawn; back to her nest alongside her sister and the seven children. Roland was left to sort through the myriad turmoils that now swirled through his head. Further rest was impossible.

For the moment, he felt euphoric. He had been enchanted by Maria since he first arrived in Darwin. And now his affection, his passion, had been returned.

But he knew that this moment of elation would shortly be engulfed by a tidal wave of guilt and remorse. The emphatic, uncompromising truths learned in the seminary made it clear that every moment of joy must be tallied against an hour of penance. You caught the biggest fish just before your boat sank. You cooked your most perfect lemon-meringue pie just before you came down with dysentery. He lay and waited to be overwhelmed by the storm of contrition, the surge of shame.

His gammy leg was hurting, probably from being asked to perform the unaccustomed gymnastics of last night. But it was a pain that brought the pleasure of recollection when it should, according to the seminary, be bringing the pang of regret. Where was the atonement? The shame didn't seem to be engulfing him as, according to the seminary, it should.

'So,' he reminded himself, 'I've stolen a truck. I've sinned against the church and I've broken enough social conventions to qualify as a pariah.'

A small twinge from his leg brought another pleasant memory. This wasn't the way he was meant to feel.

'I'm a thief,' he chastised himself. 'I've broken civil law. And I'm no longer celibate. The church won't stand for that. I'm a white man who's slept with a coloured girl. Society frowns on that sort of thing. No, worse, I'm a white priest who's slept with a coloured girl. That's a double...what? Sin? Crime?' He should be flogging himself with leather, pulling on a hair shirt, crawling over broken glass – no, his crook leg didn't allow for crawling – so, limping over broken glass. But he felt no remorse, no guilt. How was he supposed to atone for his sins if he didn't feel bad about them?

He slowly became aware of sounds, activity. Millie was raking up the fire to put a billy on the coals. A few of the kids were scuttling around the hay like puppies at play. Others stirred as they were trodden upon. As he watched, Marie sat up and stretched. She reached out and playfully tripped one of the scuttlers and then fell on him with tickling fingers until he was screeching with delight.

She glanced up at the truck, from where Roland was watching her. Their eyes met and she gave him a little, shy wave. He returned her little, shy wave. God, but she was beautiful.

The foaming tidal wave of disgrace wasted itself on the sands of infatuation. The shameless thief of trucks, the bold knight of the night, the carefree lover, climbed down from his boudoir and limped over to the fire for some porridge.

It took ten days to reach Renmark. Ten long days of grinding monotony broken only by irregular stops for fuel top-ups, meals and to stretch their legs, which had become their euphemism for a toilet break. The problem with seven youngsters was that they never wanted to stretch their legs at the same time.

The selection of overnight campsites became a consuming interest for Roland and Marie, their overriding criteria being the opportunity to continue their trysts.

Only once did their romance falter, in Port Augusta, and only for one night. They'd found a good campsite by the water's edge, near the wharf. It was the first time that the children had swum in ocean water without the threat of crocodiles and they were making the most of it by bombing off the wharf, scrambling up the rough steps and then bombing off the top again in endless repetitions. The Hannan sisters commandeered one end of the one and only warehouse for their camp and unloaded bedding and cooking gear from the truck.

One of Roland's fellow seminary students had been seconded as part-time chaplain at the nearby army camp. It was a good opportunity to catch up so, as soon as they'd finished unloading, he drove off in the truck.

He was only gone for about three hours, long enough for bangers and mash and a few beers in the army mess. It was the first time that he'd caught up with any of his mates since he'd been posted to Darwin. It was an agreeable few hours and he was in high spirits on returning to the camp on the wharf.

His high spirits were soon doused when he entered the warehouse. There was no warm greeting, no surreptitious wink. Marie was having nothing to do with him; her cold shoulder could have frozen mammoths.

That night he slept alone in the truck and next morning it was Millie who joined him on the front seat. Marie climbed into the back with the kids. Nothing was said. Even the kids seemed to sense the tension and were quiet.

They were about ten miles out of Port Augusta before Millie broke the silence. 'It's the booze, Roland. The beer.'

He looked across at her quizzically.

'You were drinking last night. Marie can't stand drinking, neither can I. That's why she 'n' me and these kids were at the orphanage. We all come from the same mob, the same settlement. Out past Rapid Creek. Everyone was on the booze, fights every night, no food. The kids were terrified. Our dad was as bad as any of 'em. Used to smack us around something awful.'

She paused and several miles went by before she spoke again. 'One night we waited until all the adults were unconscious. Then we gathered the young 'uns and walked to Darwin. Took us all night. Some coppers found us and took us to the orphanage.' Again she went silent and watched the boring landscape slide past.

'Marie copped it worse than me. She used to stand up to dad, but then he really used to lay into her. Now she just can't stand drinking, '

Roland interrupted. 'But I only had a couple of beers.'

'That's all it takes, Roland. Just a hint of booze and Marie will react.' Then she gave the faintest hint of a smile. 'I know that you two are sleeping together, known about it since Mataranka. Even the kids know. You're not much good at being discreet.'

'Ahh, bugger.'

'She's really head over heels for you, Roland. Stay away from the plonk and everything will be fine.'

They pulled over near Winninowie Siding to stretch their legs. When they resumed their odyssey, Marie had returned to the front seat and Millie was organising a sing-song in the back.

Curlew, the Riverland, 1958

The sergeant could see the Cogginses' place from his car. The big limestone house had been the first permanent building along this stretch of the river. The centre of a vast sheep run, it had, at various times, also accommodated fugitive bushrangers, a tavern, an overnight stop for Cobb & Co. and a fuel stop for the riverboats. It was one of the first properties to plant fruit trees, mostly oranges and apricots with a few rows of peaches. Melons grew in profusion behind the house and pumpkins thrived around the shearing shed.

Roland had fallen foul of the law shortly after his return from Darwin. Peter Diamond's predecessor had nabbed him when it was discovered that he was driving a stolen truck. Worse, it had been nicked from an orphanage. The magistrate had put him in the clink for a month.

That had been some sixteen years ago and Curlew had forgiven and forgotten. Nevertheless it gave the sergeant reason to regularly drop into the Cogginses' place for a look around, ostensibly to check for stolen goods. Not that he needed a reason to drop in wherever he liked. Curlew was his domain and he reckoned that gave him carte blanche to go where and when he pleased. The Reverend Douglas Trembarth and the idiots at the Police Discipline Board disagreed. It was the sergeant's unannounced and peremptory visits to the Cogginses' place that had resulted in the reminders from the board.

All but two of the orphans had left Curlew to either get married or to get jobs. The remaining pair; a lad and a lass, had married and now worked full-time on the fruit block. He was captain of the Curlew Kangas footy team and she was captain of the Curlew Cats Netball team. They were popular.

Roland had married Marie and was happy for her to run the property. Apparently she could be a right little martinet when it came to it. His crook leg had worsened so he was restricted in how much he could do around the block. He had embedded himself in the community. Much of his time was now spent as president of the Kangas and secretary of the Curlew Rotary Club. He played for the Lady Augusta Hotel darts team on Thursday nights, with practice on Monday nights. Marie didn't let him sleep in the house on Mondays or Thursdays because he smelt of beer. Theirs was, generally, a loving and warm relationship, except on Monday and Thursday nights when Roland slept in the stables to avoid the icy chill that blew through their bedroom and up his pyjama legs. It was a standing joke in the Lady Augusta Hotel and he took a fair bit of ribbing from his teammates although, truth be known, most of them quietly speculated as to whether they'd rather play darts with their mates or snuggle in bed with Marie. The general opinion was that Roland must be a lucky bugger if he needed two nights a week of rest and recreation.

Millie Hannan was chief cook and bottle-washer for the whole mob and renowned throughout Curlew as the most generous contributor of sensational cakes to any fund-raising trading table or fete. It was Millie who plundered the parishioners' gardens for her spectacular flower arrangements that ornamented the church every Sunday, except during the harvest festival, when she plundered their gardens for fruit and vegetables. The parishioners were willing plunderees.

In short, the Coggins mob was hard-working, community-spirited and popular – all the more reason for Diamond to dislike them. It occurred to him that his wife probably associated with Millie through their mutual involvement with Evelyn Trembarth and the church. He'd have to ask her about that, next time they were on speaking terms.

He started the car and took a U-turn in the car park. The diminutive priest looked up from his car-polishing and gave a cheerful wave which the copper preferred not to see and drove off down the hill. He'd cruise another lap of the town with the window down and his beefy forearm resting on the sill. Not that he expected to find any nefarious activities. He just enjoyed giving and receiving salutations from the law-abiding citizens of Curlew. It confirmed his popularity.

It irked him that the pint-sized priest polishing his stupid Wolseley had ruffled his normally peaceful tea break. It put him in the mood to annoy someone else. He might drop in on the Cogginses after he'd completed a couple of laps.

He knew his way around the Coggins place. Not surprising, he'd been making a nuisance of himself ever since he'd been posted to Curlew. One of his instructors back at the police academy had reasoned, 'Everybody has committed a bookable crime. The trick is to keep poking around until you find it, and then book 'em.' It was a philosophy that agreed with Sergeant Peter Diamond's approach to policing. He reckoned that Roland Coggins, having been pinged for the theft of a truck a few years back, was bound to have done something illegal since then. And it was a certain bet that some of his Abo mob would have broken any number of laws.

He crept the police car down the gravel driveway beside the big, return-veranda house. You didn't knock on blockers' front doors. All the activity was usually around the back.

The house, the stables and the old shearing shed formed three sides of a big courtyard, big enough to have turned a Cobb & Co. coach with a six-horse team. He parked slap-bang in the middle, got out and looked around.

The corrugated-iron shearing shed hadn't seen a sheep in years. The smell was still there along with small deposits of little black marbles in the corners. It was now used for storage of ladders and pruning tools and for the preparation of fruit for drying. Likewise the stables which hadn't sheltered a horse since the last Cobb & Co. coach rolled out of

Curlew. There were eight individual stalls all facing into the courtyard and all now missing the doors that had once kept the horses contained. The two cars and the ute that occupied the first stalls were obviously working vehicles and had all seen better days. The remaining stalls held a motley assortment of old equipment and fruit boxes. The last stall, nearest to the shearing shed, was empty but for a pile of what looked like old canvases and tarpaulins.

There were, disappointingly, no obvious stolen goods. In fact, the stuff on view wouldn't likely be nicked by any self-respecting crim.

Diamond's contemplations were interrupted by Roland Coggins. He stood in the shadow of the wide back veranda leaning heavily, but not stooped, on a solid walking stick. Marie stood close to him, arms folded. The policeman couldn't be sure if they had just emerged from the house or whether they'd been standing there all the time.

But for the stick, Coggins looked remarkably fit. Tall, lean and tanned, and not particularly friendly. He didn't leave the veranda but stepped forward into a patch of sunlight. 'Whaderyer want, sergeant?'

'And a good morning to you, Roland. And to you, Marie,' answered the copper. 'Nothing in particular. We've had reports of petty thefts from farming properties,' he lied. 'Probably the work of transients. Some of 'em look pretty dodgy. Thought I'd drop by and see if you're missing anything.'

Coggins knew that the copper was talking bullshit. And the copper knew that Coggins knew that it was bullshit. It would have been easy to fall into competitive banter but that would have required a degree of familiarity, of sociability. And neither man felt the faintest hint of fellowship towards the other.

Millie Hannan felt no such restraint. And again, Diamond couldn't be sure whether she'd just arrived or whether she'd been standing in one of the stable stalls the whole time. Bloody sneaky, these Cogginses.

She stepped into the sunlight. 'We haven't heard anything about any petty thefts. That's all bullshit. You're just snooping around like you always do.'

'And a good morning to you too, Millie,' responded the sergeant, bowing slightly. 'Actually, there –'

She cut him off and advanced on him as she spoke. 'You've never found any stolen stuff here, Diamond. That's because no one here is a thief. Why don't you find someone else to bother?'

Millie was as wide as the policeman but only about half as high. Nevertheless, she could be quite formidable when she advanced in anger. Diamond had battlefield experience with the Japanese type 95 Ha-Go light tank; all Millie needed was a coat of camouflage paint. It annoyed him that he took an involuntary step back. He tried to cover it by sitting on the car's bonnet, as if intentionally. 'Only putting out a warning, Millie. I'm telling all blockies to keep a look out for suspicious characters.' Damn, if he didn't want any more complaints from the discipline board about correct procedure, he'd have to cover his backside by warning the Cogginses' neighbours about suspicious characters that didn't exist.

'Bullshit,' shouted Millie. She engaged reverse gear and fired a departing shot. 'Bullshit!' She strode off, not easy for a short, dumpy figure, towards the shearing shed.

'Have you finished, sergeant?' enquired Coggins. 'Or do you want to poke around a bit more? Just don't dig up the pumpkin patch – that's where we bury the bodies.'

Not waiting for an answer, he and his wife turned and went into the house. The screen door slapped shut, conversation ended.

The copper eased himself off the bonnet and took a last look around before climbing back into the car. This hadn't been a good morning. Firstly it was bloody Trembarth and his bloody Wolseley and then it was this bloody Coggins pack. Bastards all.

He started the Holden but didn't put it into gear straight away, just sat there with the motor idling. Somewhere in the back of his mind a scheme was emerging like a commando walking out of smoke.

There was a note on the kitchen table when he got home: 'Bridge Club tonight. Cold meat and salad in fridge. D.'

Bridge Club. Bloody Evelyn Trembarth had introduced his wife to the Bridge Club. They met up at the church annexe, bloody church. Wouldn't be surprised if those bloody Coggins women were in the bloody Bridge Club as well, bloody Cogginses.'

He put on the kettle and, muttering inside his own head, rummaged through the fridge for the remnants of Sunday's roast. Then he flicked on the radio, sat at the pink Formica kitchen table and mulled as he ate. 'Purple People Eater' didn't improve his mood.

The Trembarths and the Cogginses, the Cogginses and the Trembarths. The roast beef was rather dry. He drowned it in tomato sauce. The salad remained in the fridge. The scheme that had been fermenting in his head all afternoon now slowly unfolded to the tune of 'Tom Dooley'. It was fully sorted out by the end of 'Poor Little Fool'. Sergeant Peter Diamond smiled through 'Volare'. It wasn't a pleasant smile.

The scheme called for the sort of backdrop against which 'Dick Diamond, Private Detective' did some of his best work: a dark and stormy night. But it was three long weeks before the weather gods decided to dish up the required conditions.

Always a topic of interest, the weather took on special significance at this time of year as summer seared through its last days and autumn promised relief. Blockers watched anxiously as the last of the apricots puckered on the long wire racks. The first hint of rain would have them scurrying to get the trays under cover before the fruit spoiled.

Of equal, perhaps greater, importance to the whole town was that Curlew was hosting the cricket grand final. It was a two-day game, and the home team had played itself into a strong position on the previous Saturday. Sitting on six for two hundred and forty-four, there had been some serious front-bar opinions as to whether Curlew should bat on or declare at the start of play. It all depended on the weather; a damp wicket would favour an early declaration.

The forecast was for storms developing during Thursday afternoon but clearing by early Friday. This was frustratingly inconclusive and served only to increase over-the-fence speculation and front-bar opinion. The captain of the Curlew Cricket Club left his phone off the hook and didn't venture into town for fear of a week-long ear-bashing.

Sergeant Peter Diamond tried to look as edgy as everyone else when ranks of blue-black cumulonimbus swelled above the northern horizon. Then he tried to look anxious as the first thunderous rumbles sent the galahs screeching from the gums and the dogs whining to be let inside.

The day had turned dark and the first fat raindrops were puffing dust from the dry earth when he left the police station through the interior door that opened into the station house kitchen. There was a note on the table: 'Show Society meeting. Sausages and salad in fridge. D.'

He screwed it up and threw it against the fridge. Then he turned on the radio to listen to the storm warnings, the flood warnings, the emergency bulletins. It seemed that the whole Riverland was in for a pounding and the radio announcer was getting quite excited by the prospect.

Sergeant Diamond went through to the bedroom and changed out of his uniform and into black. He stepped out into a screaming gale and was immediately blinded by horizontal rain. It was as dark as the inside of a black cow but he could hear the frantic thrashing of trees and the staccato ricochet of God-knows-what against corrugated iron. Infrequent stabs of lightning revealed a world of violent turmoil. 'Strewth,' he thought, 'no one in their right mind would be out in this.' The hypocrisy of his thought was lost on himself.

The road up to the church was steeper than he remembered. But then, he didn't often negotiate it on foot and into a hurricane. He carried a torch but didn't need to use it, as the lightning was increasing by the minute.

The church, as expected, was in darkness but there was yellow light spilling from one of the manse's front windows. Diamond stood and watched for a moment as the storm howled around him. At one point, the silhouette of a figure passed across the window. It was a short silhouette, probably the vicar.

There was no need to tread quietly – the raging tempest would have drowned out a marching band with bagpipes. Nevertheless, the copper, through force of habit, ducked through the garden shrubbery, commando-style, to get past the house and on to the car shed. It wasn't locked but there was a moment of concern when the wind caught the big single door, tore it from his hands and crashed it against the side of the shed. Fortunately one of the weather gods chose that exact moment to unleash a particularly impressive roll of thunder, one that would have muffled Krakatoa.

Breaking into 1935 Wolseley Hornets and bypassing the ignition had never presented a problem to car thieves back in England. Australian car thieves were untested because none of them thought that a 1935 Wolseley Hornet was worth pinching. The Curlew copper wasn't as slick as a Pommy car thief; it took him two minutes to get inside, another three minutes to get it started and less than a minute to inch it quietly past the manse, past the church and out to the road.

Once on the road and out of sight of the manse, Diamond risked turning on the headlights. Just as well. The feeble lights penetrated the chaos barely enough to show that the road was awash and littered with branches torn from the tormented gums that lined each side. The horizontal rain had now turned to hail laced with leaves and twigs that rattled against the car's windows and rendered the wipers all-but useless.

Leaning forward until his nose was inches from the windscreen, the sergeant engaged first gear and, zigzagging through the maze of fallen branches, made his way gingerly downhill, past his own police station and out to the Coggins place.

The big old house was in darkness. At almost midnight the best place to be on such a wild night was in bed. There'd be a lot of cleaning up to be done come morning, tumbled fruit trees to be propped, fallen branches cleared from roads, ruffled chickens to be retrieved. There'd be flooding everywhere.

The wind had died down a bit but the rain and hail was heavy on the corrugated-iron roof and veranda. Diamond didn't risk using the headlights but he knew the layout pretty well. There was still enough lightning to take bearings as he idled the Wolseley down the drive and into the wide courtyard. His objective was the stables, the last stall, the stall that holds only assorted rolls of canvas and tarpaulins which wouldn't make any noise if he accidentally bumped anything. The stall with room enough for a stolen 1935 Wolseley Hornet.

There was just enough room when he rammed the car into the canvas bundles and bulldozed them hard against the end wall until the engine stalled. Then he got out, gently pressed the door shut and squelched his way back to the police station and station house.

They didn't usually open the police station until around ten o'clock. Sergeant Diamond, despite not getting to bed until after one o'clock, had decided to open early. He hadn't slept much anyway. Tthe stimulation of last night's caper and the expectation of today's dramas had kept his imagination bubbling.

There was a note on the kitchen table: 'Women's Auxiliary breakfast meeting at the hospital. Eggs in fridge. D.'

Breakfast meetings! The bloody woman spent most of her time in bloody meetings. She'd been dead to the world when he'd finally crept into bed in the wee hours. And she'd been gone when he woke up an hour ago. He screwed up the note and decided on toast.

He'd expected the Reverend Trembarth to be first. The discovery of an empty shed, the theft of his beloved 1935 Wolseley Hornet, would surely have him in a right lather. It was an amusing speculation and he was whistling 'Catch a Falling Star' when he heard someone knocking on the station's front door.

It came as a surprise to find both the Reverend Trembarth and Millie Hannan on the doorstep.

'Morning, Millie. Morning, Reverend. What brings you t–'

Millie, clearly distressed, pushed forward and interrupted.

'Roland's dead, sergeant.' She choked on her own words.

Diamond had prepared himself for an amusing stolen vehicle report followed by an entertaining morning of accusations between the Trembarths and the Cogginses. Death wasn't a part of his scheme. He looked at Millie, then at the priest, then back to Millie. 'Dead?' He gaped.

The priest took a step back, shocked. Obviously their arrival at the police station together had been coincidental; they hadn't come together.

'Dead?" repeated Diamond. 'How?'

'Yes. Dead.' The little woman's voice pitched higher. 'Crushed by a car.' She pointed an accusing finger at the priest. 'His car.'

'Oh my God,' whispered Trembarth. 'My car, that's why I'm here, sergeant. To report my car stolen.' He turned to Millie. 'Millie, my God, Roland crushed? How on earth…?'

The policeman had a sudden cold, heavy feeling in his stomach. He knew what was to follow.

'In the stable,' she hissed at Trembarth. Then turned back to Diamond. 'In the stables. Where he was sleeping. His bloody car crushed him against the wall.'

Oh shit. Thursday night. Darts night. When Marie wouldn't have let him into the house because he smelt of beer, made him sleep in the stables. That's why that last stall had canvas and tarpaulins in it, that was his bedding, that's where he slept. Oh shit!

Douglas Trembarth was speaking. The policeman tried to follow what he was saying, to look attentive.

'It was stolen, sergeant. Last night, during the storm. When I went out this morning, the shed door was wide open and the Wolseley was gone. Why would it be in the stable? Who would steal it and…' He tailed off. As if an improbable thought had occurred. He looked at Millie. She shook her head as she had the same improbable thought.

'Everyone was home,' she said, calmer now. 'The storm, no one left the house.'

Another thought. This from Diamond. 'Where's Marie, Millie? Is she back at your place?'

'She went to the hospital. To get the ambulance, the doctor, somebody.'

'We'd better find her, sergeant,' suggested the priest. 'We'd better go out to…out there, and see what can be done.'

The policeman seemed a million miles away.

The priest repeated, 'Sergeant?'

'Yes, yes.' Diamond shook himself into action. He had to play this like a copper. Treat this like a real major crime, like a…what? A murder? Manslaughter? Shit! He'll have to call in the detectives from Renmark. 'Yes. I'll call Renmark. Can you two find Marie? Take her home? I'll meet you out there.'

They nodded.

He turned to enter the station and then had another thought, turned back. 'Err, best if you don't touch anything. You know, the detectives'll want, you know…'

The priest had his arm across the little woman's shoulders. 'Yes, sergeant, understood. We'll meet you there.'

Diamond stepped back into the station and locked the front door. He didn't want anyone coming in to report a missing dog or a fallen branch. He slumped into his office chair and reached for the phone. It was dead, probably due to the storm. Then he noticed Dianne standing, hands on hips, in the open doorway between the office and the station house.

'Oh, I thought you were at a meeting. There's been an acci–' he started.

'I know,' she cut him off. 'I heard it all.' She stepped into the office and faced him over his desk, arms folded. 'Someone's killed Roland Coggins.'

He paused, phone halfway to his ear. She had a strange look in her eye, bleak and bitter.

He motioned with the dead phone,. 'I've got to call Renmark. Not sure what's happened…'

'I think you are.' There was a really, really strange look in her eye, and a nasty little tight-lipped grin as she added, 'And that phone's dead.'

He put the phone back in its cradle. 'I need to get out to the Cogginses' and have a look.'

'Don't know why,' she said. Her voice was frosty. 'You were out there last night. You know exactly what happened.'

He stood and leaned towards her, hands on the desk. 'What the hell are you talking about?'

'You were out in the storm until after one o'clock this morning. Your wet clothes are still on the laundry floor. You didn't take the police car, it was out in the backyard all night.' She stepped back from the desk and pointed at him, stabbing the air with each word. 'You nicked Douglas's old car and stuck it in Roland's stable. You were trying to make it look like Coggins stole it, trying to get Douglas and Roland at each other's throats.'

'Douglas and Roland,' he thought. 'When had she got so familiar with those two bastards that she'd started calling them by their first names? Shit, she'd been socialising with those unsavoury bastards behind his back. How long had this been going on?

He pulled his thoughts back to her accusations. 'That's ridiculous. I'm a copper, I don't go around nicking cars, 'specially shitty little Pommy cars like that bloody Wolseley.' He sat back down behind the desk, reached for the phone, remembered that it was dead and folded his arms. 'What on earth would I do with a bloody old Wolseley?'

'As I said, you wanted to start a fight between Douglas and Roland. Everybody knows that you've planted evidence before. Nobody said anything because they're scared that you'd start picking on them if they dobbed you in.' She moved to the door, turned. 'That's why you can't stand Douglas and why you're always picking on the Cogginses, because they don't think that you're much of a copper. They haven't been fooled by your popular copper performance. They just reckon you're a bully.'

'That's not true,' he shouted. 'Those bastards have been –'

His wife stepped back into the office and screamed back at him, 'I saw you, Peter. You stupid bastard, I saw you. I saw you walking up to the church. I saw the old car coming down. They were all at the hospital this morning, Peter – Marie and Millie and Evelyn. Did you honestly think that we wouldn't put one and one together, Peter? We all know that you nicked that car, Peter. And now Roland's dead, Peter.'

She ran through the door, slammed it shut. He heard the lock turning on the other side.

There were other cars in the courtyard when she parked her little Ford Anglia. The Trembarths' FJ sedan was there and their 1935 Wolseley Hornet had been rolled out of the stable and sat next to the Cogginses' old Chevy buckboard.

They were all sitting around the kitchen table when she entered the big sandstone house. Teacups, pots and the remnants of breakfast suggested a happy mood. Douglas and Evelyn sat opposite Millie and Marie while Roland held court from the head of the table.

'Dianne. Come in, come in.' He laughed. 'Grab a seat, there's a fresh pot and more crumpets on the way.'

Dianne Diamond took a seat at the other end of the table. She smiled at her host. 'You're not looking too bad for a dead man, Roland.'

They all laughed.

Marie turned to her. 'He can thank the storm for that. Even I wouldn't make a bloke sleep in the stables in weather like we had last night.' She reached over the table and took her husband's hand. 'Even if he did come home smelling like a brewery horse's fart.'

'How did it go with your husband, Di?' asked Evelyn. 'Did he believe that Roland's dead?'

The copper's wife leaned back in her chair. 'In all modesty, Evelyn, I was nothing short of brilliant. I reckon I've got a future on the stage. He fell for my performance, hook, line and sinker.' She reached for the sugar. 'I might join the Curlew Dramatic Society.'

'That'd be about the only group you haven't joined,' laughed Douglas. 'I reckon that Millie and I played convincing parts too. Maybe we'll join as well.'

Roland held up a silencing hand. 'Hold on, hold on. Let's not forget the starring role. Without a corpse, you'd have had no theatre. I believe that my role was central to the plot.'

Marie turned to the vicar's wife. 'Isn't that typical of these acting types, Evelyn? Always trying to upstage one another.'

'Absolutely,' agreed Evelyn. She looked at Roland. 'Besides, yours was a non-speaking part.'

'More like a non-appearing part,' corrected her husband. Then, more seriously, he added, 'We were getting a bit worried, Dianne. You took longer getting here than we'd expected. Did he cause you any trouble?'

'Nah,' she shrugged. 'Just sat there like a stunned mullet while I locked myself in the house. I could hear him ranting to himself for a while and then he took the cop car and roared off somewhere. Then I plugged the phone back in, called the Renmark dicks and told 'em that the Curlew copper was acting all unhinged and had nicked the vicar's car. They'll be here in an hour or two to pick him up. And then I came here.'

Dianne smiled around the table. 'Any chance of a crumpet? I didn't get any breakfast at the auxiliary meeting, too much going on.'

Millie got up and fetched a plate of hot crumpets from the big wood oven. 'Do you know where he's gone?'

'No idea,' Dianne spread butter. 'And I don't care.' She took a big bite of crumpet.

For a long minute no one said anything as they considered the implications of the morning's dramatics.

The reverend broke the silence. 'It was a very clever bit of subterfuge, ladies. Quick thinking.' He shook his head and grinned conspiratorially. 'I obviously can't condone the untruths and the deceit, but nor can I condone Peter's policing methods.'

Roland stirred sugar into his tea. 'All a means to an end, Douglas. Someone had to do something. He had all of Curlew fooled. His prejudices are indefensible. He put his own popularity before all else.'

They all nodded agreement and, again, fell into silent introspection.

Marie had the last word. 'Anyway, the Renmark cops will deal with him. I suppose the discipline board will decide what to do.'

'That's true,' said Roland. 'Meanwhile, the poor bastard is driving around out there somewhere still thinking that he's killed me. I suppose someone ought to tell him the truth before he does something silly.'

Sergeant Peter Diamond wound down the window of the police car and drove with his arm resting on the sill. He swung into Commercial Street.

There was still a fair bit of water laying around and a few shops had lost some of their signage in last night's storm. A few of the shopkeepers were sweeping debris from the footpath. They paused when they saw the cop car and gave a cheery wave.

Peter returned their greetings and smiled to himself. He enjoyed being popular.

Pictures in the Window

Like so many mallee towns, Stillwell had known better days. But those better days were long past. Things had stayed pretty much the same for the last twenty-odd years and most of the good citizens were happy to have it thus.

Stillwell lived on wheat and sheep. The wheat fields, tall and flaxen-gold at this time of the year, inched right up to the edge of the rail yards on one side of town and up to the rickety back fences that loosely defined other boundaries. They were still a month or two away from harvest but only a flood, or a windstorm, or hail, or a locust plague, or kangaroos, or a wildfire, or a drop in international wheat prices, or machinery breakdown could spoil what looked like being a good year.

Remnant patches of mallee, saved only by growing in rocky gullies or other places unsafe to tractors, gave asylum to a few mulga parrots and a million rabbits. A ribbon of the stunted little trees, punctuated by haughty red gums, delineated the creek which was frequently misnamed the Nile. It was really named after its discoverer, William Nyles, but it suited the sometimes lopsided humour of Stillwell to exaggerate what was usually little more than a chain of pools connected by a trickle.

The oval, which the town shared with the one-teacher school, was once the Survey Paddock, because permanent water could be found in the steep-sided, rocky pool enclosed by a bastion of the lordly red gums. It was the only really pleasant spot in Stillwell, so it served as the venue for Sunday school picnics and the community Christmas barbecue. It was the place to sit while you waited for your turn to bat and the place for the schoolkids to gather tadpoles and wrigglers in jam jars for their lessons in nature studies. An occasional tourist's caravan, sometimes even two or three, might overnight at the pool. There was no fee and they could run an extension cord across to the power points in the toilet block, which was never locked.

The school had once boasted three classrooms but, as the population drifted away and with the advent of the regional school in Osmond, it had shrunk to just twenty students under the tutorship of one young lady who lived in the original schoolhouse. Both the school and the church, 'St Margaret's C of E', were set one street back from the High Street, behind the butcher and the bakery.

The little museum in the ex-funeral parlour, run by the Stillwell Historical Society and open on Sundays 2 p.m.–4 p.m. or by appointment, evinced that the town had started out as nothing much more than a rough tavern and stables. That had been back in the 1850s, when most mallee towns were spaced apart by the distance that a Cobb & Co. coach could travel in one day.

The next town down the line was Osmond, which had started in much the same way. There had always been a bit of rivalry between the two towns, as each strived to be something more than an overnight stop. Both had experienced a rapid population growth when Cobb & Co. surrendered their transport monopoly to the railway in 1900. Populations had mushroomed and substantial buildings – hotels, emporia, stations, banks, post offices and suchlike – lent substance and permanence.

It was the hospital that made the difference. Someone back in the capital, probably a politician with a vested interest, decided that the regional health centre would best be sited in Osmond. Then it seemed logical that the high school would also be built in Osmond. This meant that the Stillwell kids, having completed grade seven, must catch the daily bus or train to finish their schooling.

Then, as the population of Osmond swelled, commerce followed. A dentist opened his surgery, the Rural Bank moved its offices. The nearest hardware and agricultural supply outlet was to be found in Osmond, as was the only vet and the only police station.

The High Street of Stillwell became a diversity of surviving enterprise and empty shopfronts. Howarth's Railway Hotel still stood proud as the only building to boast more than a single storey, if you didn't count the modest church spire and the grim concrete grain silo looming over the rail yards. Ball's general store still declared itself to be Stillwell Emporium, while Lister's Bakery had passed through three generations of…well, bakers. Next door, Sharyn's Ladies and Gents Hairdresser only opened from Thursday to Saturday but you could arrange for Sharyn to visit you in your home if you were either incapacitated or organising a wedding.

Stone's Garage had, for three decades, occupied the rambling sandstone building that once housed the town's stables and farrier while, right next door, Harris's Pharmacy was ensconced in what had been Cobb & Co.'s booking office.

Lawrence Johns offered farm fresh meat from his butcher's shop opposite the classically pillared post office building. To supplement the limited postal business, Eric and Yvonne Field also operated agencies for the Rural Bank and AAP Insurance. Two doors down from the post office, Rex Reynolds of REX Real Estate and Property Management also found it necessary to augment his income with agencies for 4-ways Bus Lines and Alma's Stock and Station. He rarely sold a Stillwell property despite the fact that his distinctive 'For Sale by REX' signs identified unoccupied shops up and down the high street.

It was, therefore, a matter of some interest when Rex removed his sign from the vacant shop that sat between Howarth's Railway Hotel and Stillwell Emporium. It was done with an air of nonchalance, suggesting that the sale of a shop was an everyday activity for Rex. That he chose to perform his little ceremony on a Friday lunchtime, when it would be witnessed by as many people as possible, was pure coincidence.

The shop was typical: a sandstone and corrugated-iron building with accommodation in the rear and a single sales room in the front. The central, recessed front door was flanked by display windows that hadn't displayed anything but dead flies for decades. A faded and flaking shingle, still hanging from the wide veranda, testified that the last occupant had been a tobacconist.

Having removed his sign, Rex tucked it under his arm and made for the front bar in case any of the usual lunchtime drinkers had missed the fact that he had just sold a shop.

It would be diplomatic to describe Sally Howarth as statuesque. It would be risky to suggest, within her hearing, that it would need to be a bloody big statue. Sally, whose ample girth testified to the frequent sampling of her wares, had been the publican since her husband had run off with the cook. She hadn't been much of a cook, a fact neatly expressed by Sally in describing her as having lousy taste in food and worse taste in blokes.

For all of her impressive size, Sally wasn't given to coarse behaviour, nor did she tolerate it in her pub, unless it was absolutely necessary, and unless it was Sally doing it. If, in the midst of a heated football discussion, you threw a punch or let rip with any obscenities ,then you would probably find yourself drinking alone in your own kitchen until such time as Sally decided to lift your exclusion and put you on probation for six months. Some people frown on monopolies but, when you own the only pub in town, you can ignore some people's frowns. Power corrupts, but absolute power can be convenient.

Sally was happy to play along with Rex's moment in the limelight. She looked up from pulling a beer and queried, in a voice loud enough to ensure that everyone in the bar took notice, 'Sold that shop then, Rex?'

'Yer,' replied the salesman and took a pull at his pint. He was a slight and dapper man who had never been known to wear other than a natty blazer, a crisp white shirt and a trim grey fedora. When the hot, dust-laden northerlies blew into town and had everyone wearing little else but singlets and shorts, Rex remained natty and crisp. He wore a particular tie for each day of the week. This day, being a Friday, meant that he was sporting the dark blue with the thin silver stripes. The sale of a long-vacated shop had him preening like a bantam rooster.

He straightened his already perfectly straightened tie and smirked, 'Took a bit of wangling but I finally got the asking price.'

Truth be known, Rex hadn't had to lift a finger. He'd received a proposal to purchase from a Big Smoke conveyancer. The proposal had come through the mail and was accompanied by a bank guarantee and all of the necessary documentation. There was little for Rex to do other than insert his three per cent commission and post the wad of papers back to the conveyancer. No realtor had ever made an easier sale, but there was no need for Stillwell to know this.

'Good on yer,' winked the publican. 'Who's the buyer? What are they going to do with the place?'

Rex took another sip. 'No name, just Ultion Holdings, whoever they are. I've got no idea what they want to do with a vacant shop. There's a bloke coming on Monday to pick up the keys. He might know something.'

'So, what do you reckon? Might be the start of a property boom?'

This, as was intended, brought a ripple of laughter from the small group of drinkers in the bar.

'Huh,' snorted the diminutive realtor. 'Chance'd be a fine thing. I've got half of this town on my books, so a boom would be bloody welcome. Right,' he emptied his glass and pushed it back across the bar. 'I'll be off, better get back to the office and brace m'self for the boom. See yerz all later.'

A ragged response of 'See yer, Rex' followed him out of the bar as he headed for the bakery just in case Bert and Kath Lister hadn't noticed that he'd just sold a shop.

It was a good weekend. The match against Osmond was evenly balanced with Stillwell sitting on 3 for 72 chasing their opponent's first innings total of 8 for 166 declared. The ladies' tennis team made a clean sweep of their Osmond rivals and celebrated with a rowdy round of schnitzels and Chablis in the dining room of the Railway Pub. There was some passing speculation as to what was being planned for the old tobacconist's but most conversations centred on sport and wheat prices.

Rex Reynolds didn't have much time to dwell on his sales success. Saturday was race day in the Big Smoke, which meant that the office of REX Real Estate and Property Management was discreetly open to any bloke with a quid in his pocket and the need to put it on a horse. In the unlikely event of a police raid, every bloke in the smoggy little office would be found to be holding nothing other than a perfectly innocent-looking ticket for 4-ways Bus Lines. It would take the keen eye of a Sherlock to notice that each ticket had a slightly differing pattern of perforations.

Monday morning saw a professional-looking bloke park his flash-looking Ford Zodiac outside of the tobacconist's and then stroll down the road to REX Real Estate and Property Management, where he introduced himself and asked for the keys.

Rex, sporting Monday's maroon tie with little gold fleur-de-lis, accompanied him back to the tobacconist's. If he was expecting to pick up a bit of gossip about the new owner, he was to be disappointed, because the professional-looking bloke, after fitting the key into the lock, turned, shook his hand and shut the door in his face.

Sally Howarth had watched the little cameo from the veranda of her pub. She put aside her broom and whistled Rex across. 'That the new owner, Rex?'

'Nah. He's some sort of building inspector. Doesn't even know the owner. He's just going to take some measurements and organise whatever repairs need doing.'

'Hmmm. Sounds like whoever bought it is planning on opening it up again.

'Yer. Seems likely.'

'Ah well,' said the big publican as she took a few unambitious strokes with the broom, 'I reckon we'll know all about it soon enough.'

She patted her little mate on the shoulder. 'I'd better get ready to open up. See yer later.'

'See yer.'

Tuesday night was darts night. There were six teams in the Stillwell league: the pub had two teams creatively named Pub Red and Pub Blue. There was a Railways team, a Cricketers team, a Cockies team and the Churchies team.

They played in the Railway Hotel, where Sally Howarth set up two temporary dartboards in the saloon bar to supplement the two permanent boards in the front bar. Membership of each team was flexible. If a total stranger happened to wander into the pub on a Tuesday night, he was likely to be conscripted to fill a vacancy in one of the teams. Sometimes in two.

Churchies were leading the league by a country mile. Their champion, and church warden, was Peter Brabant. Easily the best player in the league, it was said that he could pin a fly to the wall across the road. Their number three player was the minister, the Reverend Devon Batt, known to the locals as Revdev. Both Peter and Revdev came under fairly critical and constant appraisal from both their wives and their congregation so Tuesday darts night became their once-a-week-hair-down-knees-up. Peter could sink beers like dehydrated camel and the reverend wasn't far behind him. In fact, Peter's accuracy with a dart seemed to improve with every pint downed. As did the volume of his already strident voice, up to a point: when he and the reverend started singing hymns in what they thought was close harmony, it was time to take them home. The trick was to organise the competition so that they played all of their games, threw all of their darts, before they started singing.

It was between games. Pub Blue had scraped home against Railways, and Churchies had creamed the Cockies. Peter Brabant's powerful rendition of 'Be Thou My Vision', with off-key harmonies from Revdev, echoed down the High Street as his victorious teammates led him home. Several of the Cockies, those of religious belief, were quietly complaining that the Churchies were getting an unfair advantage from the big fellow upstairs.

The owner of the general store and occasional ring-in for the Cricketers, Quentin Ball, sidled up to Sally Howarth as she was pulling fortifying beers for the lads from Pub Red. Quentin didn't drink or smoke. He'd been a champion athlete, represented the state in the steeplechase and the marathon and still jogged out to the eight-kilometre milepost and back four times each week. He'd kept his muscle tone and could have passed for a fit thirty but for his head, which was as bald as a doorknob. Bald blokes often attracted more than their share of nicknames – Bone Dome was typical, Chrome dome a common variation. Someone possessed of a higher wit had figured that Quentin Ball could be abbreviated to Q. Ball, which sounded like Cue Ball. This suited Quentin perfectly given that he was somewhat of a legend on the pub's pool table and that cue balls were hairless. Unfortunatel,y Cue Ball had been further abbreviated to Cuey, which kind of diminished the cleverness of the nickname.

'How's it going, Sal?'

'Good-oh, Cuey. How do you reckon your lads'll go against our Pub Reds?'

Quentin smiled. 'No contest, Sally. Your lads haven't a chance.' He paused for a moment as Sally slid beers across to the waiting drinkers. 'Listen,' he continued. 'What do you know about the tobacconist's shop? Do you reckon it'll be opened again?'

This was more than just a casual enquiry. There was discreet agreement between all of the High Street traders that no one would sell goods which were already offered by any of the others. Competition between retailers might be a good thing in the Big Smoke but it was in no one's interest to see yet another shop close down in Stillwell; there were already enough vacant shopfronts to give High Street the look of an OK Corral movie set.

So Quentin had agreed, for example, that the general store

wouldn't stock any headache powders or cough lozenges, while the pharmacists, Maurice and Beth Harris, wouldn't sell things like tissues or bicarb. The general store had the monopoly on gift-boxed fancy chocolates, the pharmacy had the monopoly on gift-boxed fancy toiletries. You could buy cigarettes in both the pub and the general store, because not everyone who smoked fags felt comfortable about buying them in the pub. But if you wanted any other paraphernalia – pipe tobacco, lighters and suchlike – then you had to go to the general store.

It was a pragmatic agreement which, like many pragmatic agreements, was probably slightly unlawful but suited everyone because it was…well, pragmatic. If the old tobacconist's was to reopen, it could upset the discreet agreement between the traders.

Sally leaned across the bar, an action that set some blokes' eyes watering. 'I'm not sure, Cuey. Shouldn't think there'd be enough trade for a tobacconist. There was a flash-looking bloke doing some sort of building inspection yesterday but he didn't seem to know anything. Apparently there's some builders due sometime next week to fix the place up. Maybe they'll know something.'

In fact, it was exactly a week later that two dusty Land Rover 109s, each towing a builder's trailer, pulled up outside the tobacconist's. The vehicles' roof racks carried lengths of timber, steel tubing and what looked like panels of substantial steel grid-work. Four overall-clad men climbed out, stretched their cramped limbs and started to unload tools and building materials.

Cuey Ball strolled over from his general store to speak with the men. 'Gidday. How's it going?'

One of the men paused from pulling a tool box from a trailer. 'Good, mate. How's yerself?'

'Yer. OK,' answered Quentin, keen to maintain the sparkling conversation. 'A few of us were wondering who's bought this place and what they're planning to do with it.'

The workman rested the toolbox on the draw bar of the trailer. 'No idea, mate. Never met the bloke. We just got a list of things that need fixing. Couple of veranda posts, door frames, window frames, that sort of thing. Check the rainwater tank and the pipes. Basically fixing and reinforcing everything.'

'So you don't know if it's going to reopen as a shop?'

'No, mate. No idea.' That said, he picked up the toolbox and followed his three mates inside.

Cuey was joined on the footpath by Sally Howarth.

'Any news?' asked the publican.

'Nah. They don't know anything about the new owner. They're just doing some repairs and reinforcing, whatever that means. There's some fairly heavy-duty timber and steel on those roof racks.'

'Bugger. I wonder if they'll be staying in the pub. Haven't had any bookings.'

'I noticed some bedding rolls in one of the Land Rovers,' said Cuey. 'Looks like they'll be sleeping in the shop.'

'Bugger. Well, maybe they'll come in for a beer. OK, I'll see yer later at darts tonight.'

Cuey lingered outside the shop for a while but the front door remained closed, so he wandered back to the general store to tell his wife that he didn't know anything. She agreed.

The builders didn't come in for a beer. They worked on the tobacconist's for five days and only occasionally did one of them venture out to buy milk from the store or pies from the bakery.

A lot of the work happened inside, where no one could see what was going on but the exterior work, replacing the veranda posts and the two big front windows, provided the townsfolk with the sort of entertainment that comes from watching someone else doing hard yakka.

Some of the replacements were mystifying: both of the big front windows had all of the glass removed and replaced by a lot of smaller and very thick panes within a sturdy grid frame which gave it the look of something out of a Dickens novel. It made the shopfront look ugly, almost guardhouse-like, and led to more speculation about the intentions of the mysterious new owner.

The builders were no help. When asked about the odd alterations, they just answered with variations on 'Don't ask me, mate. I'm just following instructions.' Late on the afternoon of the fifth day, they loaded their vehicles and left Stillwell.

The locals, adapting the Italian custom of an evening *passeggiata*, nonchalantly strolled up and down past the tobacconist's about twenty times before eventually gathering under the veranda to peer through the newly installed window with the small panes.

They couldn't see anything. The workers had hung some sort of curtain behind the glass. A quick lap of the building revealed that the small windows in the side and back walls had all been fitted with frosted glass and closely spaced steel bars. There was no way of looking inside.

It was all a bit disappointing, so most of the *passeggini* retired to the saloon bar to discuss the mystery.

'What I don't understand,' stated Beth Harris as she sipped her house white, 'is why they'd replace the display windows with those ugly-looking grille things? I mean, if it's going to be reopened as a shop you'd think that they'd want as much open display space as possible.'

'I agree,' agreed Sharyn Foxwell of Sharyn's Ladies and Gents Hairdresser. 'There wouldn't be much point in buying a shop if you didn't intend to open it. I mean, if you only wanted somewhere to live, you could buy a house. There's plenty of houses for sale around here.'

'Huh. Don't I know it,' said Rex, who had a dozen uninhabited houses on his books and hadn't sold one in the past three years.

'And the side windows are all barred,' added Sally. 'It's looking like a real fortress, or a prison. Bloody ugly whatever it is.'

'Like they – whoever – don't want anyone to get in,' said Beth. 'Or out,' she added.

'Maybe it's not going to reopen... I mean, reopen as a shop,' suggested Rex. 'Maybe they're just going to store stuff in there. Or,' he pondered, 'maybe it's a something like...like a jeweller? Yeah, maybe it's going to be a jeweller's workshop, a studio. That's why it needs all the security.'

There were a few nods.

'Could be,' said Sally, but she sounded unconvinced.

Wally Dunn of Dunn & Son, Builders, wandered in from the front bar. He had been ranting against whoever it was that had employed out-of-towners to work on the tobacconist's when he and his son could have done the job. This had raised a few discreet eyebrows from those familiar with the quality of workmanship offered by Dunn & Son, Builders. There was a joke going around Stillwell about how the local foxes had sent Wally a letter of appreciation for the quality of his chook houses.

'If he's going to live in Stillwell, then someone should tell the bugger to support us locals,' he declared in bush lawyer tones.

This was greeted with murmurs of vague agreement so he ranted on, 'And how about all the blocked-out windows and steel bars? Why's he need all that security? It's not like we've got a crime wave around here. Nothing's been flogged for years.'

'Except for the barbecue from behind the pub,' Sally reminded him.

'Well, yes,' began Wally.

'Yer,' said Stoneycold of Stone's Garage. 'And the battery charger and hydraulic jack from my place.'

'Well...'

'And the power tools from my shed,' offered Peter Brabant.

'Yer, well...'

'Someone's been nicking fencing tools from around my way,' stated Craig Matthews, pastoralist and captain of the Cockies darts team.

'Yer, well...' conceded Wally reluctantly. 'But nothing too serious. Anyway, what I'd like to know is why's everything so secret?'

'Maybe it's an international crime syndicate looking for somewhere to stash their loot?' suggested Beth, who was finding that the house white was getting better with each glass.

'Or hide the bodies?' from Sharyn.

'What bodies?' asked Sam Dunn, who had followed his father in from the front bar. Sam was the 'Son' component of Dunn & Son, Builders. Locals usually greeted him as DunnSon or SamSon and it was generally accepted that he wasn't the sharpest chisel in the toolbox.

'The bodies in the tobacconist's,' said Sharyn. Then she added 'Maybe' because Wally was giving her a stern look and you didn't take the mickey out of Sam when his dad was around. Then, to be on the safe side, she added, 'Just joking, Sam.'

Sam had been giving some thought to the mystery. 'It's a hideout,' he stated.

'A hideout?' queried Stoneycold. 'Who'd want to hide out in the main street of Stillwell?'

'Maybe a bandit,' offered Sam, whose bookshelves groaned under the weight of a hundred comics. 'Or a crime fighter, or a mad scientist, or maybe someone with a hideous deformity who has to wear an iron mask.'

'Well, yes, that's maybe a possibility,' interrupted Peter Brabant, who was getting a bit concerned that Sam's comic-propelled imagination might take him beyond the hideously deformed.

'Well,' pondered Rex. He paused to adjust his perfectly adjusted tie which, being a Saturday, meant the olive green with little silver horseshoes. 'The bloke who did the measuring up didn't know anything and the builders didn't know anything. Now that the repairs are finished, it shouldn't be long before we find out if there's dead bodies or mad scientists or bandits.'

'Or someone with a hideous de–'

His father interrupted him. 'Probably not, Sam. Just some bugger who doesn't use local tradesmen. C'mon, son, we're off home.'

The Bedford moving van had passed Quentin Ball as he was leaving on the outward leg of his early-morning jog. Two burly young men were well into the unloading by the time he got back. They'd parked around the back, in the narrow lane once used by the night-soil collectors back in the days when everyone had an outdoor dunny and needed their night soil taken away.

Sally Howarth, looking disturbingly like an over-the-hill-over-the-weight wrestler in her dressing gown, was watching proceedings as Quentin, puffing ever so slightly, joined him.

'Mornin', Cuey. Had a nice run?'

'Good, thanks. You ought to try it.'

'Huh, not bloody likely. I get puffed when I watch the footy on the telly.'

Quentin mentally sorted through the possible quips about Sally's physique. He opted for discretion and simply nodded towards the two burly blokes unloading the van. 'What's going on?'

'Dunno. Those blokes are as tight-lipped as Mafia witnesses. They had quite a lot already offloaded before I came out here.' She ran her fingers through her unruly auburn hair. 'Funny thing, though, I've not seen any furniture. It's all been nothing but those big boxes.'

They watched the yakka for another ten minutes. Sally was right, the only things unloaded were big plywood boxes. They had reinforced metal corners and were obviously very heavy. Some were managed with the aid of sack trolleys but the larger ones needed both men to manoeuvre them inside.

Quentin's wife, Valerie, joined them. Her disappointment at not being able to judge her new neighbours' taste in furniture was evident. 'Nothing but boxes!' she declared. 'Where's the beds? What about the lounge suite? No dining room setting?'

'No idea,' answered her husband. 'Maybe this is just stock for the shop. Maybe their furniture will be coming later.'

Sally shook her head. 'Shouldn't think so, Cuey. There'd be enough stuff in those boxes to stock a department store.'

A small crowd of locals had now gathered behind the tobacconist's. Sally, now conspicuous in her raggedy dressing gown, retired back to the pub. Quentin counted a further twelve big boxes being carted inside before the men closed the back of the Bedford and reversed out of the lane.

More than one of the locals quietly pondered the possibility that Beth and Sharyn might have been on the money when they'd suggested loot or bodies.

The pub's midweek order was never very big, so Lawrence Johns decided to pack it into one carton and walk it down the street rather than use his van. By the time he got to the pub, he was starting to doubt his decision. Nine kilos of schnitzels and rump steaks leaving the butcher's weighs about a hundred and nine kilos by the time it arrives at the pub.

He plonked the carton on a bar stool. Hefting it up onto the counter would have resulted in a hernia. 'Bloody hell,' he wheezed. 'That got heavier with every step.'

Sally Howarth was unsympathetic. 'Well, you buggers always weigh things so they're *just a bit over*. This might balance things out a bit.' When the only response was more wheezing, she added, 'I s'pose you reckon that you've earned a beer?'

'Yer. Thanks.'

'I may as well join you,' said the publican as she drew two pints.

It took half a pint before Lawrence was sufficiently recovered to ask, 'So, have you met your new neighbour yet?'

'Nah. No one's been near the place since all those boxes got delivered.'

'But there's someone in there now. I heard 'em when I walked past with your order.'

'Nah.' Sally shook her large head. 'You're hearing things. Like I said, no one's been near the place.'

'Well, what I heard must have been no one shifting them boxes around. I'm telling you, Sally, there's someone in there. Go and listen for yourself.'

'Bugger,' replied the big lady. 'C'mon then, we'll go round the back.'

Lawrence followed her through the kitchen and out through the rear door. They weaved through empty kegs and crates of bottles until they came to the narrow walkway that separated the pub from the tobacconist's. There was one window, frosted and barred, towards the rear of the building.

They crept up, like commandos stealthily approaching an enemy position, although creeping and stealth were not actions usually associated with over-the-hill-over-the-weight publicans.

Lawrence, a big fan of action movies, gave a series of hand signals which were intended to convey, 'Keep really quiet. You stay this side of the window and listen. I'll crawl under to the other side ,whereupon I'll stand up and take a position on the opposite side, from where I'll also listen. Be careful not to let your shadow or silhouette fall across the window for fear that it may alert whoever may be within.'

It was a very complicated set of signals which Sally read as 'I'll be picking my nose, following which I'll pretend to be a wombat before warming my ear with one hand and playing glove puppets with the other.'

In any event, the two spies, one with dirty knees, found themselves on opposite sides of the window and straining to hear any noises from within.

It wasn't easy, Stillwell in mid-morning wasn't a bustling metropolis but there were enough random noises to interrupt any stretches of silence – rubbish bin lids, doors closing, occasional footsteps, a car starting.

It wasn't helped by Stoneycold, who had a clear view of the two eavesdroppers from Stone's Garage across the street. Making a megaphone with his hands, he called out, 'Hey, Sally. Hey, Lawrence. Wot'cha doin'?' Then he tromped across to join them. He interpreted Lawrence's hand signals as 'Look at me, I'm pretending to be a traffic policeman. Now I'm patting a dog, and now I'm picking my nose again.'

But then they heard it, very faint but unmistakable. Someone was definitely moving things around. It sounded like they were being careful but it must have been difficult to shift those big, heavy boxes while trying to keep the noise down.

Lawrence, through another set of dramaturgical hand gestures, suggested that they all withdraw to the pub. Sally read it as 'You, me, him, little walky fingers, that way, up the nose yet again.' Stoneycold had it as 'Him, her, me, scratching along his arm, point, something about a nose.'

Back in the bar, Sally drew fresh pints for the blokes and poured herself a coffee. Then the three secret agents debriefed.

'No doubt about it,' said Lawrence. 'Someone's in there and they're shifting stuff around.'

'Yer, you're right,' agreed Sally. 'I'm buggered if I know when they moved in. I haven't seen anyone going in or out.'

'They might have snuck in when those blokes were delivering them boxes,' suggested Stoneycold. Then he had an idea worthy of a plot in young Samson Dunn's comics: 'Maybe they were hiding inside them boxes.'

'What?' sneered Sally. 'Tucked in with Beth's loot and Sharyn's bodies?'

Lawrence interjected. 'Look. It doesn't matter how they got in there without being seen. The fact is, there's someone in there and we need to know who it is and what's going on.'

'Why?' from Stoneycold.

'Well, who knows? They could be up to all sorts of trouble.'

'Why?'

'I don't know why. That's why we should find out. Jeez, Stoneycold, this whole business has been pretty weird. Why would anyone buy a place in the main street and then hide themselves away? Why wouldn't they at least introduce themselves to their neighbours? Why sneak in if they haven't got something to hide?'

'You're right, Lawrence,' agreed Sally. 'It's all a bit strange.' She drank the last of her coffee and rinsed out the mug in the bar sink. 'Tell yer what: why don't we just go and ask 'em?'

The mechanic and the butcher followed the publican out of the bar and onto the footpath. From there it was only twenty paces to the front door of the tobacconist's. Without hesitation, Sally knocked. It was a firm but polite knock, the sort of knock that said, 'G'day.'

There was no response. Sally waited for a minute and knocked again. This knock said, 'I'm still here and want you to answer the door.'

Another minute passed and Sally's next knock clearly said, 'Stop buggering us about and answer this bloody door.'

Absolute silence.

'Right,' said Sally. She strode up the walkway to the frosted and barred window that had recently been the scene of their furtive eavesdropping. She rapped on the frosted glass. It was a rap that couldn't be interpreted as anything other than 'Oi, you! Get out here and show yourself, you rude bloody bastard!'

But, just in case the mystery resident wasn't adept at interpreting raps, she shouted 'Oi, you! Get out here and show yourself, you rude bloody bastard!'

Nothing.

Wednesday nights were usually pretty quiet and Sally Howarth often shut the bar early.

But word had got around that someone was in the tobacconist's. And so half of Stillwell was in the saloon bar. It was buzzing. Nothing brings a small community together quicker than the fear that they might miss a juicy rumour about someone else in that small community. Or, possibly, the fear that they might find themselves to be the subject of a rumour if they weren't there.

Sally had to send word down to the butcher's that she needed another heap of schnitzels and steaks, because the dining room had been booked out. Lawrence, still nursing a crook back, brought the meat in his van. As he hauled the cartons into the pub kitchen, he exchanged eyebrows with Sally. This tobacconist's incident might be really weird, but it was bloody good for business.

The casual kitchen and bar staff rarely worked past seven o'clock on a Wednesday night but they were happy to get the extra hours and even happier to be in the middle of the Stillwell rumour mill.

As the clock approached nine o'clock, Lawrence, Stoneycold and Sally each found themselves in the centre of inquisitorial packs. It was almost impossible to hear anything against the collective din. Several rumour zealots flitted from pack to pack so as to satisfy themselves that the answers tallied. It became absurd when the wife of a local cocky asked Sally to adjudicate because Lawrence had said that he'd heard a scraping noise while Stoneycold had said that he'd heard a scuffing noise.

It was Peter Brabant who, standing tall and erect, rang a dessert spoon against an empty bottle. When a degree of peace was restored, he suggested that it would be better if the three...er...

'Stooges?' came a voice from the back.

'No,' corrected Peter. He had a very slight accent and a noticeably clipped manner of speaking. Both, he held, due to spending much of his youth working in Cape Town. 'Certainly not. It would be most appropriate if the three investigators who know most about the tobacconist's give an account of their discoveries and then take questions from the floor.'

This was greeted with murmurs of agreement from all but the cocky's wife, who thought that she had cleverly found a discrepancy in the stories and wanted everyone to appreciate her perspicacity. No one did. In fact, several members of the audience suggested that she button it while the three spies, perched on bar stools, took it in turns to describe their afternoon's doings.

'So,' Lawrence concluded, 'there's definitely someone in the tobacconists and they've got a whole lot of big, heavy crates in there with 'em.'

'Yer,' agreed Stoneycold. 'But we don't know who they are or what's in the boxes or what they're doing.'

The cocky's wife was dying to reveal another discrepancy by asking Sally whether she thought they were crates or boxes but a gritted-teeth and hissed 'Don't' from her knowing husband kept her quiet.

Peter Brabant, who had appointed himself as quizmaster, interlocutor and master of ceremonies, then opened the floor to questions by asking the first one. 'Has anyone heard anything since the scraping or scuffing noises?'

Another gritted-teeth 'Don't' kept the cocky's wife quiet while Sally answered, 'Nope. We've taken turns at the window for hours but there hasn't been a squeak.' She paused for a moment before adding, 'It's possible that my invitation to reveal himself may have been a mite insistent.'

There were several knowing nods. It was true, Sally could be a mite insistent. There was that insurance rep that tried it on with a young waitress. Sally insisted that she help him to find the front door and then she insisted that he tested the strength of her veranda post with his head. Yes, Sally could be a mite insistent.

Kath Lister, from the bakery, was a really, really nice lady. Everything about her was nice: her blonde, bobbed hair was nice, her clothes were nice, her home was nice, her whole outlook on life was nice. To know Kath was to wonder if she'd ever heard of anything that wasn't nice or whether she was aware that such things as crime or sin or naughty people existed. Her rose-coloured glasses came with optional little cherubs and fluffy bunnies. Sometimes she could be so nice that she got on your nerves. 'Do you think,' she asked in her slightly irritating, cloying voice, 'do you think that a more welcoming approach might be more appropriate? Perhaps something a little less... insistent?'

'I was only a mite insistent after no one answered,' insisted Sally. 'No one answered when I knocked on the door the first time. And it was a very friendly knock, not at all insistent.'

Lawrence nodded. 'Yer, very friendly knock. Nobody answered.'

Eric and Yvonne Field, from the post office, had enjoyed their schnitzels and were now enjoying the floor show from the back of the room. They were a quiet, unobtrusive couple so everyone turned in mild surprise when Eric called out, 'What about the meters?'

Several puzzled faces swivelled back to Peter, so he asked, 'What do you mean Eric? What meters?'

The puzzled faces swung back to Eric. One or two vertebrae clicked in complaint.

'The electricity meter and the water meter,' replied the postmaster. 'If there's really anybody in there, they'll surely be using water and power. Why doesn't someone check the meters?'

All eyes swivelled back to Peter. This seemed like a bloody good idea and was greeted with several comments along the predictable lines of 'That seems like a bloody good idea' and one or two along the lines of 'Shit, I think I've put out me neck.'

Peter sought out Rex and spotted him standing by a dartboard. 'What do you think, Rex? You're more familiar with the property than any of us. Could one of us check the meters?'

Rex straightened his perfectly straightened tie which, it being a Wednesday, was the two-tone blue diagonal stripes. 'There's no water meter. It's only got a rainwater tank that plumbs straight into the kitchen sink and the laundry. No hot water on tap. I reckon the original owners just used the wood stove to heat water. There's an electricity meter near the back door. From memory, I reckon that there's one fuse for lights in the domestic area and a separate fuse for the shop area. There's another fuse for power points but there's only about six power points in the whole place. It's all fairly primitive.'

'Thank you, Rex,' nodded Peter. 'So, if they want hot water, they'll have to either light the wood stove or use an electric kettle. Either way, we should be able to detect it.' He turned to Sally. 'I don't suppose you noticed a refrigerator going in, did you, Sally?'

It took a second for Sally to interpret Peter's clipped and accented refrigerator into a fridge. 'Nope. Just those big crates. I s'pose there could have been a little bar fridge in one of 'em.'

Kath Lister, not at all happy that the Fields had stolen her limelight, picked up where she had left off. 'I still believe that we should try a more welcoming approach,' she syruped. 'I propose that we make up a nice little welcoming basket to leave on their front stoop and slip a nice little greeting card through their front-door letter box.'

'Not such a bad idea,' suggested Rex. 'When they open the door to get the basket, we should be able to get a glimpse of them, or maybe even start chatting.'

'That's right. Maybe they're just really shy.' Kath's smile was so bright that it was painful. You half-expected her to clap her little hands together and say 'Goody, goody.'

'And,' added Rex, 'while you're distracting them with your cards and baskets, I'll sneak a look at the meter.'

Peter addressed the throng. He knew that he cut an impressive figure when he addressed throngs. He was relishing his role, which was much more exciting than chairing the church council. And it came with beer and schnitzel and a much bigger throng to address. 'Well, everybody, we haven't got any answers but I suggest that we try Kath's welcome basket plan and Eric's electricity meter plan and see what happens.'

The general murmurs of agreement encouraged him to go on. 'I'd like to propose that we appoint a small residents' committee to coordinate everything so that we don't get twenty schemes all happening at once.' And then, because it didn't pay to leave these things to chance or democracy, he added, 'If I may be so bold, I'd like to suggest that the committee be comprised of Sally, Quentin, Rex and myself. All in favour?' A few slowly half-masted hands were enough. 'Right, then. That's carried.'

Kath spent much of the following morning flitting up and down the High Street and popping into every shop to gather nice little donations to pop into her nice little welcome basket. She found it amazing how generous everyone was, how quickly they handed over their donations and, consequently, how little time she needed to spend in each shop.

Quentin and Valerie Ball, for instance, seemed to have anticipated her arrival and already had a nice little selection of biscuits and chocolates waiting on the counter. She hardly had any time to chat about the local mystery before Quentin called Valerie to the back of the shop to help with something.

She had barely entered the pharmacist before Beth Harris dropped several bars of nice soap into her basket. Kath hardly had time to say 'Thank you, they're really ni–' before Maurice called from the back of the shop to help with something.

Lawrence Johns had a nice little bottle of mint sauce waiting on the counter of the butcher's shop, Sharyn Foxwell had some nice little sachets of shampoo and Yvonne Field had a nice little stationery pack waiting in the post office.

Rex met her on the footpath with his nice hot-off-the-press REX Real Estate and Property Management calendar for next year. Paul Stone also offered a calendar from Stone's Garage but it wasn't, in Kath's opinion, as nice as Rex's. Frolicking kittens were nice but a topless young lady draped over a tractor tyre definitely wasn't. Kath accepted both calendars but discreetly decided that whoever was hiding in the tobacconist's probably wouldn't be needing tractor tyres.

She finished her harvesting in Howarth's Railway Hotel, where Sally added a nice little bottle of Irish Crème Liqueur that had been sitting on the top shelf since last Christmas. '

That's a nice little collection you've got in there,' Sally said as she poked through the goodies. 'You've done nicely.'

Kath beamed. She sometimes thought that people didn't appreciate her niceness so it was extra-nice to get a bit of praise from the rambunctious hotelier. 'Why, thank you, Sally,' she dripped. 'Everyone has been really nice.'

'It's really quite pathetic,' thought Sally in a rare moment of warmth. 'That's ni– That's great, Kath. Tell you what, why don't you nick off back to the bakery and tell your husband that he has to mind the shop. Then hop over the road and grab Rex and then both of yer come back here and we'll knock up a few schnitzels for lunch and make plans.'

'Oooh, Sally. That sounds nice but I'm not sure.'

'Bugger that, Kath. You've done a ni– A good job this morning. Here, we'll have a quick pre-schnitzel sherry and then you go and tell Bert that we've called an extraordinary meeting.'

The plan was finalised over veal schnitzels and a reasonable sauvignon blanc. Kath and Sally would push the welcome letter through the letter slot and then make as much noise and fuss as possible as they put the welcome basket on the front-door stoop of the tobacconist's.

While that was going on, Rex would quietly make his way to the rear of the building and check the electricity meter.

The best place from which to keep an eye on the welcome basket would be the pub's veranda. It was slightly higher and a little further forward than the tobacconist's veranda, so an observer could keep a watchful eye on things without being easily seen. Sally drew up a roster for the four elected committee members and then had to amend it to include Kath who, having found herself to be unaccustomedly acceptable, insisted on taking her shift.

The afternoon and evening shifts were most agreeable, sitting on a warm veranda with a cold beer wasn't an onerous duty.

Cuey, loitering outside his general store, instructed any passers-by not to dawdle as they passed the tobacconist's. 'Don't look at the basket,' he advised. 'Just keep walking past as if nothing was going on. Act natural.'

Everyone followed the instructions and walked, naturally, past the tobacconist's. Everyone walks naturally, it's in their nature to walk naturally. But if you ask someone to walk naturally, they become focused on walking naturally which, because they don't usually focus on their natural gait, becomes unnatural. So the passers-by, concentrating intently, adopted a range of perambulations that included the string-puppet, the crab-shuffle, the stiff-arm-military-march and the Olympic-hip-swivel. Having negotiated the tobacconist's veranda, they further spoilt the intention by quickly crossing the street to gather on the opposite footpath just outside Stone's Garage.

By early evening, a crowd of thirty or more was assembled in anticipation of someone emerging from the tobacconist's to collect the basket. Each, in their own way, tried to act naturally. But a congregation of thirty people, each acting naturally but facing the same way, didn't look collectively natural. An angry Sally crossed the road from her pub and used her insistent voice to disperse them.

The undercover agents convened on the pub veranda, where they debriefed over steak sandwiches. Rex reported that the electricity meter was static;, no power was being used by the mystery inhabitant. He'd taken note of the readings just in case he might need to compare them against future scrutiny.

Sally reported that the residents who had gathered outside of Stoneycold's were a bunch of dickheads. Cuey agreed.

Kath reported that the steak sandwiches were really nice and that she'd had a really nice day and was looking forward to pulling her one-hour shifts during the night.

The short summer night passed uneventfully. The welcome basket remained on the tobacconist's stoop and no noises were heard from within.

Kath, disappointed at the lack of response to her welcoming gestures, trotted off early to help her husband at the bakery. The three men also headed home, leaving Sally to keep an eye on things from the pub.

Stillwell slowly woke up. Sunrise brought a dry northerly that rattled a percussion of loose corrugated iron and teased strips of bark from the gums. A few regulars called into the store for milk and newspapers and to listen to Cuey's account of the night watch. Several customers offered suggestions as to what the next step should be. The majority view seemed to involve kicking the door in and sorting the bastard out.

The pub had more pre-lunch customers than usual, although most of them only stayed for one small beer. It didn't take Sally long to figure out that the small beers were just an excuse to walk past the tobacconist's and check the basket. At least that was preferable to congregating on the footpath and gawking from across the road like a mob of emus watching a lizard.

Lunchtime was busy and all the talk was about baskets and tobacconists.

The spy ring met in the early afternoon and agreed to keep watch for another night. It was Kath who suggested that the chocolates in the basket wouldn't have improved for being left on the footpath on a hot day.

And so another night passed with nothing to show for it. Kath, who felt that her second stint at surveillance hadn't been quite as nice, again left early to help with the Saturday baking. Rex left shortly afterwards to organise Saturday's regular SP bookmaking operation, while Quentin jogged off to get in his sixteen kilometres before it got too hot.

Peter Brabant and Sally were left drinking tea in the pub's kitchen.

Sally had been working her usual pub hours on top of her night watch shifts. She felt as wrung out as a trainer's towel. 'Well, Peter. So much for Kath's welcome basket. Whoever's in there wasn't interested.' She groaned as she rose from the table and took their cups to the sink. It was a fair effort to shift herself at the best of times; she felt heavier when she felt fatigued.

'Tell yer what, Pete. I'm going to catch a few zeds before opening up. Would you mind collecting the basket and dropping it back to the bakery?'

'Certainly, Sal. And I'll organise a meeting for early next week. We'll see if we can decide on what should be our next plan of action.'

It was Cuey's insistent banging on the pub's back door that got Sally out of bed far too early on the following Tuesday.

She appeared, bleary and tousled and barely contained within her dressing gown. 'Bloody hell, Cuey. It's barely six o'clock. What's up?'

Quentin was in his jogging gear: shorts and T-shirt. Sally was about to pass judgement when she noticed his grim expression. The tone of his voice matched his bearing.

'You better come and see this, Sally. In the window next door.'

'Why? What is it?'

'Best just come and have a look. It's really weird.'

'Hang on then,' she said. 'I'll throw on some clothes.'

She reappeared, just minutes later, in slacks and a big, floppy cardigan which, to Quentin's eye, wasn't much of an improvement on the dressing gown. He said nothing and led her to the front of the tobacconist's.

And there, in the remaining front window, and supported by a sturdy-looking easel, was a painting.

It was a large painting, probably a bit over a metre and a half across and a bit over a metre high. It was nearly as big a painting as could fit in the front window.

'Oh, jeez, ' uttered Sally and then stood in silence alongside Quentin as she took in the scene before her.

It was a painting full of figures, lots of people crowded along a table, a celebration of some sort. Other people were standing or carrying things. Their clothing was from another time, a long time ago. It was rustic-looking, jerkins, tight breeches, wimples, cloth caps. Her attention was drawn to the two dominant figures, two men carrying a big wooden plank – no, not a plank, it was an old door supported, stretcher-like, on two long handles and doubling as a convenient way of carrying things. It was a busy painting, full of movement. The colours were mostly earthy, rural, but with a few splashes of strong red on clothes and caps.

For a fleeting moment, Sally found herself considering that it wouldn't look bad on the wall of the pub's dining room. She also found it to be, somehow, slightly familiar.

Quentin brought her back. 'Look at the faces.' It was half-whispered, as if in a gallery where paintings must only be discussed in half-whispers.

Sally leaned forward slightly to change her view from the all-encompassing to the specific. 'Bloody hell.'

She knew every face. The two men carrying the old door were unmistakably Wally and Sam Dunn of Dunn & Son, Builders, just as the figure in the bottom corner, the one with the basket, was unmistakably Kath Lister. She had never seen Paul Stone in tight white leggings and red blouse but the painted figure standing behind the Kath Lister duplicate was clearly Stillwell's garage proprietor. He was pointing at the objects being carried by Wally and son. Deeper into the scene stood a man apparently looking into some sort of cabinet fixed to the wall. It was Rex.

'Bloody hell,' she muttered as she studied the revellers seated along the refectory-style table. Every face belonged to a citizen of Stillwell. There was the slightly gaunt face of young Janette Wilson, the schoolteacher who always tugged on her earlobe when speaking, just as depicted in the painting. And there was the railway overseer, Don Something-or-other, never came into the pub and was too old to think that he could get away with a Beatles haircut.

Four of the carousers were local Cockies with their wives. Revdev was occupied with an industrial-sized tankard and, alongside, Maurice and Beth Harris seemed to be well into their cups.

'Jeez.' Sally stepped back and turned to Quentin. 'They're really well painted, Cuey. I mean, you can recognise every face. They're almost like photographs. Even some of the gestures and expressions are spot on.'

'Too right,' agreed Quentin. 'Whoever painted this certainly knows what he's doing. But it's not just the faces, Sal, it's the details. Take another look at Rex. Wha'der yer reckon he's doing?'

She peered again at Rex. Then she turned again to Quentin. 'Bloody hell, Cuey. He's reading the bloody meter!'

'That's right. Now cast your mind back to when he did it, and take another look.'

She did. And when she straightened up and looked again at

Quentin, she was pale. 'Oh, jeez, it was last Thursday, and he's wearing his Thursday tie. The grey one with the dark red stripes.' She paused and looked again. 'Shit, Cuey. Look at Kath's basket.'

'Yer. I know. Everything that she'd collected is in there, except for Stoneycold's calendar, see? It's lying on the ground next to her.'

'Bloody hell.'

'Look at the plank-thing that Wally and Sam are carrying. There's bowls of food on it like you'd expect. But there's also other stuff – there's power tools and a battery charger. Do you remember that Peter had power tools nicked out of his shed?'

'Yes,' murmured Sally thoughtfully. 'And Stoneycold had a battery charger knocked off from his garage. And there he is, Cuey. In the painting, pointing to it on that plank-thing that Wally's carrying.'

She stepped back from the window and put a hand to her mouth. She turned wide eyes on the storekeeper. 'Jeez, Cuey. Do you reckon that... ' She paused, unable to fully come to grips with her own conclusion. 'Do you reckon that this bloke, this artist, do you reckon that Wally and...'

'I do, Sally,' answered Quentin and put a steadying hand on her shoulder. 'I reckon that this artist is telling us that Wally and his boy are the bastards who have been knocking off all the stuff that's been going missing.'

'But how, how would he know?'

'Sally, whoever did this painting, he knows this town, he knows everyone in it. Christ, look at the faces, they're perfect. They're not just faces, they're portraits. He knows all about the welcome basket, even Stone's calendar. He knows about Rex sneaking a look at the meter.'

'Jeez. This is really weird, really scary. This is...' Stuck for words, she shook her tousled head. The confidence that comes with a large physique was lost, replaced by the vulnerability that comes with total uncertainty. 'Oh hell,' she managed. 'I need a drink.'

'You're buying,' Quentin smiled grimly, all thoughts of jogging long past.

By mid-morning you couldn't walk past the tobacconist's. Not that anyone tried to; they were all too busy trying to push to the front of the crowd that had gathered under the veranda.

Few of them understood the inferences presented by the painting; they were more intent on seeing whether they could spot their own face somewhere in the composition. The regional weekly newspaper, the *Mallee Tribune*, relied on that same need for self-recognition. Its strong circulation figures came not from its brilliant reporting but from cramming each page with group photos of choral societies, or junior cricket teams, or Rotary Club meetings or netball presentations. People bought the newspaper if they thought that their face might be in it. The most scrutinised texts in the *Mallee Tribune* were those studied by photographees checking that their names were spelt correctly in the captions.

Nobody in the crowd seemed overly curious about who did the painting or how such accurate portraits could be achieved. Their only concern was whether or not their faces were on display. The general buzz of interest was punctuated by little squeals of 'Oh look. There's Doris,' or 'There I am, next to Don.' There were also grunts of discontent: 'Why on earth would anyone want to paint Doris?' and 'That's her, next to Don, always pushing herself forward.'

Matters were taken far more seriously by the committee meeting in the pub. Paul Stone, reasoning that he was central to the painting, invited himself to join them. They didn't include Kath because of the awkwardness about her unilateral decision to exclude Paul's calendar, the one with the topless lady and the tractor tyre.

Peter Brabant, a firm believer in the natural order, assumed the chair. 'Well, there is a lot to discuss and many questions to be answered. Perhaps the first to be answered is why that painting seems so familiar?'

'I've got the answer to that,' said Quentin Ball as he ceremoniously laid a thick book on the table. He opened it to a page marked with a strip of card. 'This is Valerie's,' he explained somewhat apologetically.

'She did a semester of art history at teacher's college. She recognised the picture straight off. It's called *The Peasant Wedding* and it was painted by Peter – no, hang on, by Pieter – Bruegel sometime in the 1550s.' He swivelled the book so that everyone could see the illustration. 'It's really clever how it's been adapted by our artist. A lot of the heads have been swivelled a bit so you can see the faces.'

'And this corner is where Kath is holding the basket,' pointed Sally. 'But here in the original it's a bloke pouring drinks.'

Paul Stone had stood to get a better look. 'That's me in the middle,' he leaned over Sally's shoulder to point. 'What's that gadget that I'm holding?'

'They're bagpipes,' offered Quentin. 'He's one of the musicians at the wedding feast. But our artist hasn't put in the bagpipes, he's got you pointing to your battery charger instead. Here, it's on this plank thing.'

'Along with my power tools,' added Peter. 'And they're all being carried by Wally Dunn and his son. Does anyone here question the obvious implication that the Dunns are thieves?'

'It surely looks like it,' sighed Sally. 'But I'd like to know how he knows.'

Quentin shrugged. 'Seems to me that our artist has gone to a lot of trouble to show that he knows what's going on. He's got Kath with her basket and Rex with the meter box and all the other faces, all really accurate portraits. I reckon that he's proven that he knows all about us just so's he can point the finger at Wally.'

'Still doesn't tell us who he is or how he knows so much about us,' added Rex. 'But I agree that he's telling us that Wally and his lad are thieves. So what should we do about it? Call the coppers?'

'Are the coppers likely to believe a painting?' asked Sally.

'Probably not,' said Rex. 'So all we have to do is invent a likely story that throws suspicion on the Dunns.'

Peter turned to him. 'Are you suggesting that we lie to the police?'

'Yep, nothing easier. Paul reports some stolen items and I report that I saw Wally sneaking around Paul's garage late at night.'

'And then what?'

'And then the cops go around to Dunn's place and find some stolen items?'

'And what if the cops don't find any stolen items?' asked Paul.

Rex sighed. He was going to have to spell it out. 'Have you replaced that battery charger that they nicked?'

'Yes, but…'

'Then we take your new battery charger around to the Dunns' and leave it where the cops can't miss it.'

They all pondered on this for a few moments before Quentin said, 'You know what, Rex? You're a devious little bastard, aren't you?'

'Thank you,' grinned Rex. 'That is praise indeed. And might I remind everyone that I have managed to avoid any police interference to my little Saturday enterprise? My credentials as a devious little bastard are well-founded.'

'But how do you propose to sneak the new battery charger into the Dunns' premises?' questioned Peter. As a pillar of Stillwell's society, he was feeling reluctant to become involved in Rex's nefarious activities.

'They're not there,' offered Sally. 'They're working on a shearing shed a hundred kilometres up north. Some poor sod who hasn't heard about their shonky building practices.'

Rex spread his arms wide. 'There you go. Easy. I'll get the battery charger sorted and first thing tomorrow Paul can call the cops.'

It turned out to be easier than they could have hoped for.

There were two coppers based in Osmond. One was Senior Constable Garth Staker who, rumour had it, had been busted down from sergeant for some rather unsavoury behaviour back in the Big Smoke. His posting to Osmond was to serve both as a penance and as an opportunity for the air to clear a bit before he returned to city. As a result, he was an angry man with a chip on each shoulder and enough prejudices to fuel a Klan.

The second cop was Errol Clements, an open-faced, straight-out-of-the-academy lad who, his instructors had decided, would probably last about five minutes on the city streets. In fact, young Clements had that sort of bland countenance that was known to incite normally mild people to violence. More than one instructor had felt a knuckle-tingling urge to smack him around for no other reason than to wipe that gormless expression off his face.

Those same instructors, in recommending Clements's posting to Osmond, had failed to appreciate that he would probably last about five minutes with Senior Constable Garth Staker. What little self-confidence remained in young Clements had been, in fact, exorcised by Staker in about two minutes. Blessed with an expansive wit and an enviable mastery of the language, the senior constable had managed to convert 'Errol' into 'Ear Hole' and from there to 'Wet-behind-the-earhole'.

The Osmond police were meant to visit Stillwell for at least one half-day each week. No one was quite sure why. Possibly to ensure that insurrection hadn't broken out or that an international diamond-smuggling syndicate hadn't established its headquarters in the disused hardware and gift shop next to the butcher's.

Senior Constable Garth Staker held the view that Stillwell was a more backward backwater than Osmond and, as such, not worthy of a visit by his awesome self. On receiving Paul Stone's complaint about a stolen battery charger, he ordered Junior Constable 'Wet-behind-the-earhole' Clements to investigate. His parting words, delivered in what he thought was a really amusing twangy hillbilly accent, were 'And don't let yourself be flummoxed by any of those inbred, two-headed, banjo-playing yokels. Just write a report and get out of there before they marry you off to one of their hogs.'

This was, however, the junior constable's first solo assignment, his first opportunity to practise detection. He would get to the bottom of this crime even it meant learning the banjo and marrying a hog.

And so it was a very determined young copper who pulled up outside Stone's Garage in the green Land Rover with the police insignia on each door. He would have much preferred the newly delivered HR Holden patrol car but Staker had staked his claim on that.

There are several ways by which a determined but untried junior copper can mask his uncertainty. Junior Constable 'Wet-behind-the-ears' Clements opted for the impenetrably coolly efficient because this was the style preferred by the better class of detective novel.

Paul Stone greeted him on the footpath and offered his hand. Clements, caught in the act of removing his notebook from the pocket of his tunic, made a mess of the handshake and then dropped the notebook, and then his biro.

Stoneycold, who had been nursing some misgivings about lying to the police, put aside his doubts and decided to play this young copper for the twit that he was. 'Good to see you, officer,' he lied. 'We're getting sick of this pilfering, so it's a relief to see the law stepping in.'

'Oh?' queried young Clements, ace detective, as he dropped his notebook again. 'So you've had other thefts? You've not reported them previously?'

'Well, no. Didn't want to waste valuable police time on a few minor incidents. We know how overworked you protectors of law and order must be, Osmond being the HQ of the Mallee Mafia.'

The young Dick Tracey made a quick note to follow up on the Mallee Mafia before asking, 'When you say "we", are you suggesting that others have had items stolen?'

'Oh, yer. Sally's lost a gas barbecue, Pete's had tools nicked, '

'And none of this has been reported?' More notes.

'No. Like I said, didn't want to waste your valuable time. But this time we've got a witness and we reckon that we know who the thief is.'

'And who,' questioned the young Ellery Queen, 'who is this witness?'

'That'd be Rex. He's in the pub. Follow me.'

That said, Stoneycold strode across the High Street with the young Peter Gunn following in his wake and trying to write in his notebook at the same time.

Sally, watching from behind the dining room curtains, reported to the rest of the committee. 'Hah, it's that junior copper. The one they call Wet-behind-the-earhole. He's about as sharp as his own truncheon.'

They spun their story to the young Sherlock and gave him descriptions of the pilfered items. Sally gave him an old photograph of the Pub Red darts team gathered around the gas barbecue before it was stolen. Scribbling furiously, he filled ten pages of his notebook.

After twenty minutes, he left for the Dunns' place. He was smugly satisfied that his interrogation technique had extracted every shred of information. Rex, the informant, was smugly satisfied that the young Hercule Poirot had swallowed his bullshit story hook, line and sinker.

The young Charlie Chan returned an hour later. He was just in time to witness the committee finishing the last of their steak sandwiches. This reminded him that he'd skipped breakfast and was late for his lunch. There was no offer of a free steak sandwich which, he told himself, was just as well because he was not open to inducements.

'So,' quizzed Rex. 'Find anything?'

'I certainly did,' answered the young Adam Dalgliesh. He consulted his notebook to remind himself of what he had written three minutes earlier. 'I located your barbecue, Mrs Howarth, and there are a number of power tools that seem to fit your descriptions, Mister Brabant. I actually found two battery chargers, Mister Stokes. One of them looks near-new.'

Rex and Paul exchanged glances. 'So what do you propose be done, constable?' asked Peter.

'Well, I'll need to bring my colleague, Senior Constable Staker, up to speed. Then I'll require each of you to make a positive identification of the stolen items. Meanwhile, I'll be issuing a warrant for the Dunns' arrest.' He flipped his notebook closed and stuck it into his breast pocket, missed, and retrieved it from the floor. 'Right, I'll be off. Thank you for your cooperation. I'll be in touch.'

That said, the young Inspector Clouseau got into his Land Rover, stalled it twice and then drove off.

It had been an entertaining interlude but the joke didn't last.

It was Rex who brought them back to the mystery as they took coffee in the dining room.

'Does anyone have any idea how long it would take to paint a picture like that?'

There were general shrugs of cluelessness around the table.

'Why do you ask, Rex?' queried Peter.

'Well, it's been less than two weeks since that furniture van unloaded those crates into the tobacconist's. I can't see how anyone could knock up such a complicated picture in under two weeks.'

They considered this for a moment.

'You're right, Rex,' said Stoneycold. 'There's got to be nearly twenty portraits in it. Takes forever to paint a portrait. I saw some bloke on the telly painting the queen, took him months.'

They all turned quizzical looks on the garage owner, who had never previously shown any leaning towards the world of art appreciation.

He caught their puzzlement. 'I was flicking through channels during the tea break,' he explained. 'England was 3 for 68.'

They considered this for another moment.

'I suppose that most of it could have been painted beforehand,' pondered Quentin. 'He could have already painted the people sitting at the table and the Dunns carrying the loot.'

'Yes,' agreed Peter. 'And then all he would have to do was paint Kath and Rex to establish the accuracy.'

'Which tells us,' said Rex, 'that this person has spent a lot of time in Stillwell before he actually moved into the tobacconist's. He already knew about the Dunns' thievery and he already knew exactly what everyone looks like. Strewth, this just gets weirder and weirder.'

Sally gathered up empty coffee cups. 'But why? Why would he buy a shop and pay to get it fixed up and then hide away like a criminal and then whack a bloody great picture in the window? I mean, if all he wanted was to dob in the Dunns, then he could have easily done it without all of the expense and all of the mystery.'

They nodded. They'd all had the same disturbing thoughts.

'If you ask me,' offered Rex, 'this isn't the end of it. That painting was put in the window to establish his credentials, to tell the whole town that he's got us marked. This bloke knows a million times more about us than we know about him. You have to wonder what the bastard's planning to do next.'

On that sombre note, they all went home.

Sometime during that night, *The Peasant Wedding* was removed from the window. Quentin was first to notice its absence when he set off for his early morning jog.

'So the Dunns' thievery is exposed and the painting is removed, job done!' he thought to himself. And then he thought again, 'No, not done. I reckon the bastard's just started.'

Friday passed without incident. Few people seemed interested in the exposure of the Dunns. Even fewer seemed impressed by the incredibly convoluted cleverness that brought about their exposure. Mostly they wanted to see if their faces were still in the window.

Saturday morning saw the usual influx of cockies' families intent on weekly shopping, socialising and picking up their mail. A steady trickle of blokes dropped into REX Real Estate and Property Management, where they bought bus tickets and listened to the radio.

At the end of the day, Stillwell had made 227 in their first innings and had Osmond looking down the barrel at 4 for 50 in their second dig. Most of the team gathered in the front bar for beers and celebratory steak sandwiches. The tennis hadn't gone so well, so the ladies settled down to an evening of commiseration schnitzels and consolation Chablis in the dining room. Thoughts of tobacconists and paintings and thievery were set aside in favour of runs scored, rubbers lost and horses winning.

Stillwell slept in on Sunday morning. That is why the first to notice the new painting in the window were Quentin and Valerie Ball as they made their way to church with their three children.

It wasn't as big as *The Peasant Wedding* nor was it a scene of merrymaking. There were only three figures and they were lying on the ground in postures that suggested lascivious drunkenness.

Only one face was immediately recognisable. It was the

schoolteacher, Janette Wilson. She was lying face-up and with her thin legs spread widely. One bare arm was flung out and her clothes were dirty, dishevelled and barely providing a degree of modesty. Her expression was one of vacancy, eyes glazed, mouth hanging slightly open. It was impossible to think of any way that the artist could have made her look any worse, any more slovenly or licentious.

Church forgotten, Valerie Ball thought only to shield her three children from the appalling image and to protect the schoolteacher from the public view. She had sometimes been called upon to act as relief teacher at the little school and probably knew Janette Wilson better than anyone else. They had never been friends; Janette was too distant, too uncommunicative to call a friend. But there was a professional bond in their shared training as teachers.

Hustling the children back to the general store, she called back to her husband, 'Quentin, get a bed sheet or something, and some tape. We've got to cover that thing up.'

She returned to find her husband taping magazine pages to the individual small panes of glass that had replaced the original single large window.

'Now we know why those builders were told to install this framework,' he said as he tore another length of tape from the roll. 'It's to stop anyone smashing their way in. The steel frame is like a cage.'

His wife joined him and held the paper sheets as he taped them to the panes. Several other curious churchgoers, drawn to the Balls' frantic activity, craned around them to glimpse the obscenity on display. They were gently but insistently eased aside by the bulk of Sally Howarth, who had noticed the gathering from the pub's veranda.

'Morning, Valerie. What's going on, Cuey?'

'Have a look at this,' said Quentin as he pulled a corner of a magazine page from a windowpane.

Sally pressed forward to study the painting. There were several complaints from the bystanders as her substantial frame blocked their view.

Unconcerned, she took several minutes to absorb every detail of the offensive picture. 'God,' she finally whispered as she stepped back, 'that's awful. Here, give us some of that paper. Let's get it covered.'

When they had covered those panes that offered a view of the painting, Quentin turned to his wife. 'Did you recognise the painting, Val? Is it by the same artist – what's his name? Broober?'

'Bruegel,' corrected his wife. 'Yes, it's in the book. I can't remember its name but it's definitely by Bruegel. Let's go inside and I'll look it up.'

They headed for the general store, leaving a disappointed gathering standing under the tobacconist's veranda. Quentin locked the front door while Valerie fetched her big book of *The Late Renaissance Outside of Italy*.

She flipped through pages of Holbein, Altdorfer and Bosch before arriving at Bruegel. 'Here it is. *The Land of Cockaigne*.'

'Cocaine?' questioned Sally and Quentin in unison.

'Not sure,' said Valerie. 'It's spelled differently. Hang on...' She read a few lines. 'No, apparently it refers to general gluttony. Not drugs as such. The three people in the picture have been pigging out until they can't move.'

'But the Janette figure,' asserted Sally. 'The Janette figure is surrounded by hypodermic needles and glass pipes and stuff. All things used by druggies. Did you notice the strap wrapped around her bare arm and all the dark blotches on her skin? They've got to be needle marks.'

'I was too busy covering it up to take in the details,' said Quentin. 'The way that she's posed is bloody disgusting enough. Flat on her back, legs spread, bloody disgusting.' He turned to his wife. 'What's she like, Val? I've only ever passed the time of day with her when she comes into the shop, never really spoken to her. You've had more to do with her, with your relief teaching and such.'

'She's pretty good with the kids, doesn't let them get away with much. Her paperwork is sloppy, doesn't always get the administration stuff done. I've seen a few reminders from the regional office.'

'What's she like? I mean, when she's not teaching?'

'Not particularly friendly. Kind of distant and vague, not what you'd call outgoing. I don't think she's very happy to be stuck in Stillwell. Strikes me as a real city girl, doesn't like us country bumpkins.'

Sally was studying the book. 'There're some weird details here. Look, there's a pig with a knife stuck into it and a chook half out of a pan. Looks like a whole lot of pies or tarts on a shelf back there and a boiled egg with…feet?'

Valerie studied the picture. 'Yes, all symbols of gluttony. Bruegel often included little touches of surrealism. But there's no drug paraphernalia, no needles or anything. Our artist has added them.'

'And the three figures lying down,' pointed Sally. 'Two of 'em are plump, like overfed. But the Janette figure in the painting is really skinny.'

'She is,' agreed Valerie. 'I mean in real life, she's really thin. Doesn't look after herself, doesn't eat properly. Sometimes she looks absolutely washed-out and gaunt.'

'Like a drug addict?' suggested Quentin.

Valerie considered this for a moment. Not many people in Stillwell had much experience with drugs. They read a lot about it in the newspapers but most of the stories came from the Big Smoke. She knew that the young teacher didn't spend her weekends in Stillwell, that she couldn't wait to clear out as soon as possible on Friday afternoons and didn't get back until late on Sunday. She was one of those transients, the schoolteachers and the bank clerks who either stuck around on weekends and joined local sports teams or who spent as little time as possible away from the big city. Janette was one of the latter.

'Well,' she conceded, 'when you put it like that, I suppose yes, she could be taking drugs.'

'So, do we call in the constabulary again?' pondered Sally. And then she answered her own question. 'No, probably not. We've got nothing to show except for a painting in a window. We don't know if Janette is actually taking drugs or, if she is, whether she's using them here in Stillwell. So, what should we do?'

'Nothing much that we can do,' offered Quentin. 'It's not like we can set ourselves up as a local vigilante, run her out of town. As Sally says, we've nothing but that offensive painting. I reckon that the best that we can do is keep the window covered up and find an opportunity for one of us to have a discreet little chat with her before the whole town gets involved.'

His wife nodded. 'Meanwhile, we better open up the shop. People will be knocking the doors down for their Sunday paper.' She unlocked the front door and took the 'Open' sandwich board to the footpath. She was back within two seconds. 'Better have a look at this.'

Quentin and Sally joined her. There was a small crowd standing in front of the tobacconist's window. Torn magazine pages littered the footpath. A few scraps of tape still hung from the window panes but, otherwise, the painting was in full view.

'Bugger,' said Quentin. 'So much for keeping it a secret.'

The general store only opened for two hours on Sunday mornings. Enough time for Stillwell to buy the Sunday newspaper and an extra litre of milk to see them through the weekend.

On this particular Sunday, the Balls might as well not have bothered. The pile of newspapers on their counter barely diminished. No one was particularly interested in the printed news; they were far too engrossed in the painted news in the tobacconist's window.

Quentin was just about to lock up when Eric Field, the postmaster, stepped inside. Eric was a compact man, slightly under average height and slightly over average weight. He wore his thinning, gingerish hair cut very short, which gave his head a blurrily gilded edge in the backlight of the morning sun. He, like most of Stillwell, had spent a compellingly outraged ten minutes taking in every detail of *The Land of Cockaigne*. Then he'd felt so overwhelmingly disgusted with the depraved image that he had spent another five minutes checking that he hadn't missed anything.

Eric was, as well as postmaster, the chair of the school committee. The entire committee consisted of just five members and met once a month to fulfil the requirements of the Education Act. They were meant to oversee the quality of learning being delivered to the children of Stillwell and the maintenance of the tiny school's facilities. No one could remember a meeting going longer than about fifteen minutes due partly to the fact that everything seemed to be going along quite well and partly because the teacher, Janette Wilson, could be a bit unnerving. Nothing you could put your finger on, nothing to make you think that she was anything but a competent teacher. No, just a sense that you'd feel more comfortable if you weren't sitting around the same table as her.

The normally calm and unflappable Eric was in a flap. 'Valerie, Quentin,' he vibrated without preamble. 'What can we do about this…this outrage?'

'Yes,' agreed Valerie from behind the counter. 'It's a vicious painting.'

'Well, yes. It's terrible, terrible,' shuddered the postmaster. 'But what I mean is, the drug-taking. What are we going to do about Janette Wilson's drug-taking?'

Valerie placed both hands on the counter and leaned forward. 'Hang on there, Eric. We've got no proof that Janette takes drugs. That painting doesn't prove anything. You can't go around accusing people of things just because some weirdo puts it in a painting.'

'But that last painting,' protested Eric, 'the one with Wally Dunn in it. The cops proved that it was right, didn't they? Everything in that painting was right on the money, wasn't it? This artist bloke knows all about us. He knew about Wally and I reckon that he knows about Janette.'

'So what do you propose?'

'Well, we'll – that is, someone will – have to confront her, get to the truth of the matter,' stuttered the chairman. He rather enjoyed being chairman but not if it meant using the chair to fend off lions.

Valerie sighed. 'By "we", I hope that you mean the school council.

I'm not a member, so don't include me. Janette usually gets back to Stillwell fairly late on Sundays, so you'll have time to organise your committee and decide what you're going to do. Now, if you don't mind, we're going to close the shop and have lunch.'

That said, she escorted Eric to the door. As he reluctantly left, she glanced towards the tobacconist's and the gathering of art critics. 'Jeez,' she thought. 'I reckon that Janette is already being judged guilty without a trial.'

There was a better-than-even chance that their Sunday afternoon would be anything but relaxing if they stayed at home, so they packed a scratch picnic lunch, not a difficult task given that they lived in a general store full of tucker, and headed for the Nile.

Their two boys chose to ride bikes. They'd zoom ahead and then return to circle their parents and younger sister before zooming off again. It was less than half a kilometre from the store to the pool but the boys covered it in five kilometres.

The afternoon was cloudless and bright. A benign northerly was content to swish the tops of the big red gums but couldn't find enough energy to raise dust. The idyll of the Nile pool was being shared by several similarly minded families. Each had spread tartan blankets in the patches of shade and the balmy air was punctuated by a recital of tadpoleing, French cricket and bikes.

The boys tore off on a lap of the oval while Quentin added his blanket to the patchwork. Valerie watched on as their daughter applied herself to the serious business of unpacking the picnic hamper and selecting which of the temptations were to be exclusively hers and which might be shared with her brothers.

They had a clear view across the oval to the school, where a farm ute was parked near the gate. A second was just pulling up.

'That'd be the gathering of the school council,' suggested Valerie as she sliced a metwurst. 'I'll bet that Eric's already inside.'

'I'd like to be fly on the wall,' smiled Quentin. 'Or perhaps not...'

Skippy was bounding across the grainy screen when the phone rang. Valerie rather enjoyed Skippy. Not so much the actual programs, which she found to be as predictable as porridge and as unlikely as... well, as unlikely as an intelligent kangaroo. No, what Valerie enjoyed was watching her kids watching *Skippy*. She could tell, by watching their animated faces, whether the scene being played out on the screen was one of happiness, or sadness, or tension or, best of all, one in which the bad guys got their just deserts.

So the ringing of the phone interrupted Skippy's urgent dash through the bush to raise the alarm about those ignorant campers' untended campfire.

'Bugger,' she said to herself as she made for the hallstand and picked up the jangling intrusion. 'Hello...'

The bushfire had been extinguished, the culprits well and truly chastised and the opening fanfare of the nightly news had sent the kids scurrying out of the lounge room by the time she hung up.

Quentin came in from the storefront. 'Who was that on the phone?'

She sighed. 'Eric. Asking if I was free to put in a couple of days' relief teaching. Janette's shot through.'

'How do you mean shot through?'

'Gone. Left. Shot through. Apparently Eric and the committee were waiting for her when she arrived at the schoolhouse. They questioned her about the drug-taking.'

'And...?'

'And she told them, in no uncertain terms, what they could do with the school, and with Stillwell in general. Apparently her language was quite colourful and quite explicit as to where she told them to stick it. Then she just grabbed all of her stuff from the schoolhouse and stuffed it in her car and shot through.'

'So, are you going to fill in tomorrow?'

'Not much choice, is there? Eric's going to contact the regional office and organise something more permanent. He reckons that they won't get anything sorted until the end of the week, so it looks like I'll be filling in for a few days at least.'

'Ah, well, Christmas isn't too far away. The extra cash will be useful.'

Valerie nodded. Then she paused before looking at her husband. 'There's another thing,' she added pensively. 'Eric was worried that the regional office might not give us a permanent replacement for Janette. The school's barely big enough to warrant it. He reckons that this little drama might give them a reason to shut it down and bus the kids to Osmond.'

That night *The Land of Cockaigne* was removed from the window.

Nothing short of an alien invasion could put a stop to darts night. The drama and subsequent departure of the schoolteacher was the subject of speculative conversation between games but the focus of the evening remained fixed on scores and beer. Peter Brabant, Rex Reynolds and Quentin Ball managed to consult with each other and with Sally between games and between pulling beers for the rowdy players.

The storekeeper gave a summary of Sunday's events and ended by adding Eric's concerns about the possible closure of the school. 'It's all about economics,' he stated. 'Whether it's cheaper to employ a teacher for only twenty students or cheaper to run a bigger bus to Osmond.'

'But surely, Cuey, it's better to teach the kids in their own town?' asked Sally as she pushed four beers across the counter to the victorious captain of Pub Blue. They'd just knocked off Railways and the win had moved them up to third on the league ladder.

'I'm afraid that what's best for the kids doesn't always make economic sense,' said Quentin. 'There's already a school bus that picks up a handful of high school kids and some of the younger kids on farms between here and Osmond. It would only be a matter of putting on a bigger bus. It wouldn't cost the department much more.'

'Well, there've been rumours about the closure for as long as I can remember,' offered Rex. 'I suppose this drugs business has only served to remind the regional office about us. Seems like it's a borderline case. We could probably fight it.'

'Maybe,' reflected Peter, who had been following the conversation between turns at the dartboard. 'But if we had a drop in student numbers, it would be a certainty. There might be a few parents prepared to pull their kids out because of the drugs issue.'

He was summoned back to the game, which was proving to be a bit touch-and-go with the number one player from Cricketers. He needed fifty-two for a win.

'Twelve-double-top,' advised Revdev unnecessarily.

The first dart missed by whisker and stuck a five.

'Forty-seven,' came another unnecessary bit of mathematics from the reverend. And then, annoyingly, 'Nine-double-nineteen.'

Peter's next dart nailed the nine but his final shot landed just below the double-nineteen.

'Thirty-eight to win,' cried Revdev as he chalked it on the scoreboard.

The Cricketers player took his stance. He needed sixty-one. Nineteen-fourteen-double-fourteen was, possibly, the best option, so Revdev called out the less-likely 'thirteen-eight-double-top' just to sow a seed of indecision into the opponent's mind. There was nothing in the Ten Commandments about darts, so the reverend had no qualms about a bit of applied psychology

It worked. The Cricketers' number one followed Revdev's doubtful advice and jagged the required thirteen with his first arrow. But then he had to switch his focus to the opposite side of the dartboard to where the eight beckoned. The odds of hitting the triple-eleven were inconceivable but that is just what he did.

'Fifteen required,' announced Revdev, trying not to sound too gleeful. 'Three-double-six,' he offered.

The Cricketers man successfully nailed the required three with his third dart and then stepped back to allow Peter to take his stance at the line. He needed a double-nineteen and he jagged it with his first dart. The players shook hands and the victorious Churchies captain rejoined his fellow committee members at the bar.

Rex had followed the game from his perch on a bar stool. He swivelled back to take a pull from his glass. 'This bastard in the tobacconist's is certainly stirring the shit, isn't he?'

Quentin nodded. 'But he's not breaking any laws and, so far, he's been right on the money.'

'True enough,' said Sally. 'First the Dunns and now the teacher. It's almost like he's playing sheriff, like he's set out to clean up this one-horse town. Like he's the community conscience.'

'And I suppose...' said Peter, 'I suppose that the issue of the school closure is coincidental to his crusade to expose our lawbreakers. I mean, I don't believe that he would intentionally cause the school to close. I can't see how that would serve any purpose.'

He had cause to reconsider this statement when the next painting was revealed on the following morning. It was a parody of another Bruegel; *The Peasant Dance*. There weren't many peasants on display, but there were a lot of Quentins and a lot of Sharyn Foxwells in various stages of intimacy. A lot of the foreground, where Bruegel had placed a dancing peasant couple, was filled with a semi-naked Quentin prancing with an equally semi-naked Sharyn. There were barely enough scraps of underwear to maintain a modicum of decency but it looked as if one more shimmy would have it down around their ankles.

Even those unfamiliar with Quentin's nether regions could hardly mistake the athletic build and gleaming bald head. Sharyn's rather generous proportions, just slightly enhanced by the Dutch master, were equally recognisable. Nevertheless, the artist had ensured that their faces were turned in such a way that there could be no doubt as to their identities. Nor could there be any supposition that it was only by chance that Quentin had gone cavorting in his undies in the near vicinity of Sharyn, who had, by chance, felt a similar urge to strip down to knickers and bra and have a quick jig.

Any doubt as to their identities would be quickly resolved by the discovery of a second Quentin in somewhat closer ballet with a second Sharyn in the background. Again, their state of déshabillé could not be misinterpreted.

On the other side of the canvas, the artist had added a final, and undeniably intimate, third Quentin and third Sharyn locked in the act of kissing. Central to the composition was a musician, a bagpipe player. It was Paul Stone. He was fully clothed in peasant's shirt and leggings. In fact, all of the remaining figures – the other dancers, a trio of argumentative drinkers sitting behind the musician and the assembled onlookers in the background – were all fully and modestly clothed in mid-sixteenth century peasant garb. It was this backdrop of normalcy that served to highlight, as if such was necessary, the blatant display of carnal immodesty presented by the multiple, and fleshy, couple.

The flesh and blood Quentin was normally a sound sleeper so he wasn't sure why, on this particular Wednesday morning, he had woken earlier than usual. He lay awake for several minutes listening to the sonorous breathing of his still-slumbering wife.

Then he heard a faint tinkling from outside. He'd heard it before. It was, unmistakably, an empty bottle rolling across concrete.

'Bloody cats,' he thought as he eased out of bed.

Valerie's regular breathing faulted in protest. 'Whad's?' she mumbled.

'Bloody cats knocking over the empties again,' he replied as he started pulling on his jogging togs. 'Still early. You might as well stay there a bit longer.'

'Ahhhh, no,' sighed Valerie. 'Might as well get up. I might head over to school a bit earlier and get a few more things sorted.' That said, she rolled her feet out of bed and sat on the edge, ruffling her hair and yawning.

'I'll give that bloody cat a kick up the arse before I head off,' said Quentin. 'See you when I get back.'

'I'll probably be gone by then,' advised his wife. 'If the kids aren't ready for school by the time you get back, give 'em a hurry up.'

'Right. See you.'

It took him about fifteen minutes to reorganise the crates of empty bottles on the back veranda. It was difficult to imagine that a cat could have scattered the bottles and crates so far and wide. 'Must be a bloody big cat chasing a bloody big mouse,' he pondered, and then thought nothing more of it. The day threatened to warm up rapidly and the eight-kilometre post beckoned.

He jogged slowly, enjoying the still-crisp morning air. The bitumen was striated with the shadows of the thin, multi-trunked roadside mallee. Occasional kangaroos, lurking in the shadows, took evasive bounds out of his path and then, knowing him not be a threat, stood in bemused diversion to watch him pass. Corellas, tinged yellow by the sunrise, rasped their way overhead. For a kilometre or two, he was accompanied by two kookaburras flying a little ahead of him to announce his progress.

As he turned for the homeward leg, it was noticeably warmer and he picked up the pace a bit so that he'd have plenty of time to check that the kids were all set for school.

There were no kids to check on. There was no wife. The family's Ford Falcon station wagon was gone from its usual home under the backyard carport. The back door was wide open.

Quentin's curiosity pushed a dozen possibilities through his mind. Maybe Valerie had decided to take the kids to school in the car? But it was only a five-minute walk to the school. Maybe she needed the car to take stuff to school? But she hadn't brought any work home from school; it was easier to stroll over there and do whatever needed doing on-site.

Then a few nasty scenarios suggested themselves. What if someone had broken in and then stolen the car? Or worse, what if something had happened to one of the kids and Valerie had to rush them to Osmond Hospital?

Feeling a rising panic, he pushed through the doorway and into the kitchen. It was unusually messy, the sideboard littered with breakfast remnants, one chair lying on its side and cupboard doors open. He failed to register that the large volume of *The Late Renaissance Outside of Italy* lay incongruously on the kitchen table and opened to a half-page illustration of Bruegel's *The Peasant Dance*.

'Hey. Anyone here?'

No answer.

He strode into the lounge room and found clothes strewn over the furniture. 'Hey,' louder. 'What's going on? Anybody here?'

Their bedroom was a chaos. Wardrobe doors hung open, drawers had been pulled from the dressing table and dumped on the unmade bed, their contents scattered.

The kids' rooms were much the same, wardrobes emptied and clothing scattered. The linen press in the passage hung open and there were empty spaces where things had been removed. Why would thieves take towels?

Now in an absolute panic, Quentin pushed through the door that connected the family quarters to the general store. The first thing that he noticed was that the till was open and there was no money left in the drawer. So, a robbery? He quickly checked the emergency secret stash that they kept in an innocuous biscuit tin pushed to the back of the counter shelf. With the nearest bank now in Osmond, most Stillwell businesses kept a fair amount of cash on hand. It too was gone. But no one knew about the stash except Valerie and himself. Had they forced her to reveal it? How?

He scanned the shop, the sense of dread now near-unbearable. The lights were on but the front door of the shop was still locked. So the thieves had entered through the house? There were things on the floor; someone had grabbed stuff from the shelves, not caring that other things were being strewn underfoot, soap, toothpaste. Why would thieves take toothpaste?

Other things: the glass-fronted freezer was empty but for a landslide of frozen meals cascading across the floor and now thawing into a puddle. There were gaps where cereal packets should be and biscuits and, God, so much food was taken.

He stumbled to the front door and drew back the bolts and the deadlock. The bundle of morning papers lay waiting, as they should, on the stoop. Ordinarily Valerie would have already carried them inside.

Stepping over them, Quentin was momentarily dazzled by the morning light so he didn't notice Sally approaching until she was almost upon him.

'Oh, Cuey…' was all she managed until he grabbed her by the shoulders and stammered, 'Sally, something's happened. Valerie and the kids, Valerie and the kids aren't here, Sally. Something's happened. Someone's taken them, Sally. There's stuff – clothes, Sally – everywhere…' The words were barely audible through his trembling.

Sally grabbed him by his upper arms and shook him firmly. She hissed into his face, 'They're all right, Cuey. They're just gone. You stupid bastard, Cuey, they're gone. They've left you, Cuey, you stupid bastard.'

He shook his head in blank misunderstanding. 'What? What do you…?'

She shook him savagely and then, grabbing him by one elbow, propelled him roughly to the tobacconist's window. 'Look, Cuey. Look, you stupid bastard. That's why Val and the kids have shot through. Look at it.' The last words were shouted as she shoved his face into the window panes.

She left him staring at the lewdness on display and then, noticing the approach of several spectators, advanced on them like a Matilda tank. They retreated as she insisted, as only a large and angry lady publican can, that they might 'Piss off and keep out of this, you nosey bastards.'

Quentin turned away from the window. He looked crushed. 'Sally, where're Valerie and the kids?'

'I'm buggered if I know, Cuey. I heard a bit of a commotion out the back of your place and, when I came out to see what was going on, she was loading up your wagon with boxes and cases and stuff. The kids were carrying bundles of stuff too. Then she got them into the wagon and they…they just went.' She pointed to the window. 'And then I came around to the front to see where you were. And then I and saw this. Obviously Valerie had already seen it. Jeeze, Cuey, what the hell's been going on with you and Sharyn?'

'Nothing, nothing,' he groaned. He sagged back against the

window and then, almost as if he had been burnt by the image on the other side of the glass, lurched forward. 'I mean, nothing since… Ohhh, jeez, Sally, it was ages ago. It was just one time, it was, I dunno, a year ago? Jeez, it was only one time.'

'Well, the whole town's going to know all about it before long, Cuey. It's not going to matter if it was only once or a hundred times. Everyone's going to reckon that you're a shit, Cuey. And that includes me.' She turned to walk back to her pub.

'Sally,' he pleaded.

But she turned and pointed straight at him, finger like a pistol aimed at his head. 'You're a shit, Cuey. This is all about you being a bastard. Why don't you just piss off back to your shop and lock yourself in and figure out what the hell you're going to do about it.'

This time, she didn't try to stop the spectators who were gathering just beyond the range of her invective. They began edging, ever so gradually, towards the tobacconist's window. She pushed roughly through the nearest of them on her way to the pub.

Peter Brabant and Rex Reynolds arrived about ten minutes after Sally phoned them. 'You'd better get over here,' she'd announced without elaboration. It hardly needed elaboration. It was obviously another painting.

On the way to the pub, they'd both taken a minute to push through the protesting onlookers and see for themselves.

There was coffee waiting in the dining room. They sat around the only table that didn't still have chairs perched on top in preparation for the morning's vacuuming.

'Jeez, ' began Rex. 'Who'da thought that Cuey and Sharyn…? I mean, how long has this been going on?'

'He reckons that it only happened once, about a year ago,' answered Sally. 'Seems like the only person who knew about it is that bastard doing the paintings.'

Peter's clipped manner of speaking seemed even more staccato.

'And we still don't know who he is or how he knows so much about the town, or about the people who live here.'

'Where's Cuey now?' asked Rex.

'I told him to lock himself back in his store,' answered Sally. 'I've no idea where Valerie and their kids have gone. They took off in a hurry.'

They drank coffee in silence for a long minute.

'Hell, Cuey and Sharyn,' mused Rex. 'How does a bloke who's as bald as a beach ball hit it off with a hairdresser? I mean, there's not much in common…' he tailed off in realisation that this was, probably, an inappropriate time for humour.

'Yer, well,' said Sally, 'I'm told that opposites attract.' She paused to pour more coffee. 'The thing is, it only happened once and nobody knew anything about it until this bastard exposed it in that hideous painting. Obviously Cuey regretted it enough not to keep his little fling going, and Sharyn's kept it under her hat. It's not some sort of clandestine affair, just a bad mistake.'

'But now it's out there for everyone to see,' broke in Peter. 'What do you think Cuey will do? And Sharyn for that matter?'

Sally's answer was interrupted by a sharp rapping on the door. She rose to let in an agitated Bert Lister.

'Where's Cuey?' he demanded without preamble.

'Sit down, Bert. Here, have a coffee,' offered Sally. 'Cuey's in his store.'

'Is it true that Valerie and their children have left Stillwell?'

They all nodded.

Bert continued, 'Is she coming back?'

'Shouldn't think so,' answered Sally. 'They packed a fair bit of stuff, clothes and suchlike. Why do you ask?'

'Well, she's doing the relief teaching until we get a replacement for Janette. There's no one else available, there's no one to teach the kids tomorrow, Oh, shit!' He looked at them aghast. 'Oh, shit,' he repeated, and looked at his watch. 'There's no one there to teach the kids today.'

'Well, you'd better get over there, Bert,' said Rex through a humourless smirk. 'This is what being the school chairman is all about:

crisis management.' His last words were all but lost in the slamming of the door as the school chairman headed for his crisis.

Peter was first to realise another consequence. 'You know, if Valerie doesn't bring her three kids back to Stillwell, it could be the end of the school. They'll close it for sure.'

'Strewth,' said Rex. 'I hadn't thought of that.' He stirred his coffee absently. 'Is it drawing too long a bow to believe that the bastard in the tobacconist's has targeted the school? I mean, first he gets rid of the teacher and now he's managed to reduce the number of students.'

'But he wasn't to know how Valerie would react to Cuey's adultery,' suggested Sally. 'She could have done anything. I reckon that we're giving this bastard artist too much credit.'

'I'm not so sure,' argued Rex. 'He's been right on the mark three times so far. Jeez! What's that?'

'That' was a loud commotion from outside. Peter led the other two out of the pub's front door. The spectators at the tobacconist's were being treated to an additional floor show as Quentin attacked the window with a spade.

'Get, out, here, you, bastard.' He swung the spade with each word.

A spade is not a housebreaker's first choice of implement; an axe or sledgehammer would have been more appropriate. So the spade was largely ineffectual as Quentin's haphazard blows bounced off the steel frames, causing more sparks than damage. There was a scratch in one of the small glass panes but, otherwise, the wildly brandished implement threatened to injure the spectators more seriously than the window.

'Strewth,' muttered Rex. He made to step forward but Sally put a restraining hand on the little man's shoulder.

'Hang on, Rex. Here come the Johnny Hoppers.'

The small group of onlookers had grown to become a decent crowd of spectators which now included several schoolchildren. Apparently, Chairman Bert had handled his crisis by closing the school and sending the kids home. They had prudently moved back out of the range of Quentin's wildly flailing spade. Now they moved even further back to watch as a new HR Holden police patrol car swung into the kerb with an impressive squeal.

Senior Constable Garth Staker emerged and took a moment to take in the scene and to give the audience an opportunity to take in his impressive self. He was a large man – tall, broad-shouldered and broadly paunched. An imposing and bristly moustache separated a veined nose from a thin-lipped slit of a mouth that seemed permanently shaped to displeasure. Deep-set grey eyes glowered from between heavy brows and multiple bags.

He lifted his cap from the front seat and screwed it onto his large head. It didn't help: you can't disguise ugliness by adding officialdom.

Senior Constable Garth Staker not only hated the mallee, he unreservedly loathed it. There was nothing about the mallee, or the countryside in general, that SC Garth Staker didn't abhor. He hated his posting to Osmond which, although chronicled as a regional centre, still clung to its affiliations with things like trees, and sheep, and crows.

No, SC Staker was a city cop through and through. He was at home with vice, and corruption, and kickbacks, and graft, and bribery. Truth was, it was his intimate familiarity with, and occasional participation in, these activities that had earned him his current posting to the mallee.

Some itinerants learn to blend, to assimilate. Not Staker. He still thought of a fence as someone who received stolen goods rather than something to keep the sheep in. And while weed to a farmer was an unwanted pest, in the city it was a cash crop.

And, while he found Osmond to be abhorrent, the disgust with which he viewed backwaters like Stillwell knew no bounds.

He observed the mob of local yokels silently gawking as one of their number attacked a shop with a spade. This observation did little to dispel Staker's contention that mallee folk were a sausage short of a sizzle.

'Right, you,' he bellowed from his classic copper's stance alongside the police car. 'Put down that...' He paused, unsure whether to call it a spade or a weapon. 'Put down that spade', while factual, didn't sound very authoritarian. 'Put down that weapon' didn't sound appropriate since it was, undeniably, a spade. He settled on 'Put that down,' and then, by way of added command, 'Now.'

Quentin swivelled round. His bald pate glistened with sweat, his eyes red-rimmed and wild. The conventions of televised cop shows demanded that his response should be along the lines of 'Come and get it, copper' as he advanced with weapon or, in this case, spade, raised in a death-dealing manner. But Quentin was buggered, so he just dropped it.

Senior Constable Staker proceeded to mount the veranda and grabbed the exhausted storekeeper by an arm. Then, also abiding by the conventions, he kicked the spade out of reach lest the criminal grab it and shoot someone.

Having secured the criminal, Staker was a little uncertain as to how to proceed. As a city cop, he hadn't encountered many gangland killers wielding spades nor, for that matter, many extortionists attacking shopfronts. His usual manner of proceeding was to knee the criminal in the crutch and then kick him in the ribs before throwing him against a brick wall and rasping something conventional like 'You're finished, dickhead,' or 'Let's do a deal, dickhead.'

But this was different. Applying a knee to the crutch of a breathless, sobbing storekeeper who had done nothing other than remove a few flakes of paint from a window frame…well, even in Staker's eyes, it might be seen as a tad excessive. He was saved from a potentially disastrous exercise in public relations by the advancing bulk of Sally Howarth.

'Good morning, senior constable.' There are several ways of pronouncing 'constable'. Subtle inflexions and accents can impart various levels of respect. Sally's was dripping with a lack of it. 'We rarely see you around here. What brings you to Stillwell this morning?'

'Anonymous tip-off,' growled the copper as he habitually sized up this apparent adversary. He could usually judge, to within millimetres, where best to aim his knee. But Sally was as large as he and lacked the…the necessary anatomy to be incapacitated by a knee. This gave him yet another uncomfortable pause for thought.

'Anonymous tip-off, senior cont-stable?' repeated Sally loudly and with even more emphasis on the 'cont-stable'. 'And what did this anonymous tipster tip you off about?'

'A disturbance here, in Stillwell.'

She turned slightly to ensure that the local yokels wouldn't miss anything. 'And how long ago did you receive this anonymous tip?'

''Bout an hour.'

'Ahhh,' smiled Sally. 'And yet this disturbance, assuming that your anonymous tipster was referring to Quentin's little tizz, this disturbance only started about fifteen minutes ago. So your tipster is also able to predict disturbances that haven't started yet?' This brought an appreciative snigger from the local yokels who knew Staker by reputation and found his actual presence to be even more disagreeable.

'Don't know about that,' said the big man, who now found himself preventing a sagging Quentin from slumping onto the ground. 'But I do know that this bloke was smashing up the front of this shop. That's a disturbance in anyone's book.'

Sally turned to the spectators, the defence lawyer addressing a jury. 'Buggered if I saw him smashing anything. No broken glass anywhere. He hardly managed to hit anything, let alone smash it.' She turned back to the copper. 'Why don't you take a look at the picture in the window and judge who's really at fault here?'

'Right. Here, take this.' He handed Quentin to Sally, who effortlessly took the shopkeeper's subsiding weight. Then he proceeded to look in the window.

Senior Constable Garth Staker was no art connoisseur but he knew near-nudity when he saw it. He squinted at the painting from several different angles as if he might get a glimpse of something better than merely-nearly-nudity. It took him some time, therefore, to look beyond the nearly-nude bits to the faces.

Realisation slowly dawned across his disappointed dial. He turned and pointed at Quentin, and then back to the painting and then back to Quentin again. 'That's him, isn't it?'

'Well done,' grinned Sally as she took a fresh purchase on the increasingly flaccid storekeeper. 'I can't imagine why you've never been promoted to detective.'

Another ripple of appreciation from the gallery didn't go unnoticed by Staker. He chose to ignore it, or, rather, to file it away for later.

'Who's the bird?'

'The bird, cont-stable, is none of your business. The point is, cont-stable, that this painting is slanderous and indecent. If you're going to arrest anyone for creating a disturbance, cont-stable, it should be the mongrel who painted it.'

Staker had not enjoyed the past few minutes. These yokels, these… these country bumpkins, were proving to be a bit sharp, a bit uppity. Particularly this big bird from the pub. He'd be scrutinising her attention to the licensing rules in future. But for now he saw an opportunity to stick it back to them. 'Nothing indecent about it,' he judged. 'All of the offensive bits are covered.' He pointed again towards Quentin. 'You'd see a lot more in some of them magazines that this bloke's probably selling under the counter.'

Quentin, who had partially regained use of his legs and was slowly progressing from limp to leaning, interjected, 'I've never sold those…'

Sally interjected his interjection. 'You've got the wrong storekeeper, cont-stable,' she enunciated. 'This bloke has never sold anything more offensive than *The Women's Weekly*. There's the cause of the ruckus.' Quentin had recovered sufficiently to be semi-self-supporting so Sally was able to free one of her arms and point to the tobacconist's window. 'That bloody painting is downright slanderous. You ought to arrest the bastard.'

Staker shook his large head. 'Not a criminal offence, slander. That's civil, that is. You want to ping him for slander, you get yourself a lawyer and trot off to the civil courts.'

Rex had stepped forward to help keep Quentin vertical. 'But we don't even know who the bastard is,' he shouted in frustration. 'How are we supposed to sue him if we don't know who the hell he is?'

Staker grinned maliciously. This was better. These bastard bumpkins were getting their knitting in a knot. 'Not my problem. There's nothing illegal about displaying a perfectly decent painting in a window. Not a bad painting either – good likeness to Sonny-Jim here, even with his knickers around his knees.'

Sally and Rex made to interrupt but Staker held up a hand to keep them silenced. 'Tell you what,' he smirked, 'seeing as how there's been no damage done, I'll let Sonny Jim off with a warning this time. But,' he raised his best authoritarian voice to a level that could be heard halfway to Osmond, 'but, if I hear of any more disturbances in Stillwell, I'll be down on all of yerz like a ton of bloody bricks.'

He paused to strike another despotic pose and swivelled slowly to ensure that every onlooker felt the threat in his stare. That done, he removed his hat and carefully reached through the Holden's window to place it on the passenger seat. Then he strode around the bonnet, opened the driver's-side door and gave everyone a final baleful look before easing behind the wheel.

His audience was silent and transfixed. He milked the moment by slowly adjusting his rear-view mirrors, slowly adjusting his seat belt, slowly flicking an invisible dust mote from the windscreen and then, and only then, starting the engine. Then he slowly selected reverse, checked every mirror for any unlikely slowly approaching traffic and then slowly reversed into the street. Then he slowly selected first gear and took forever to drive out of sight.

There was a collective exhalation.

'C'mon, Cuey,' said Sally. All of the anger she had felt towards Quentin had now been spent on the copper. 'Let's get you inside. We could all use a drink.'

Sometime during the night, *The Peasant Dance* was removed from the window. It was replaced by *The Misanthrope*.

'So what is a misanthrope?' asked Rex.

Sally had borrowed the big *The Late Renaissance Outside of Italy* from Quentin but he hadn't joined them in the pub. He hadn't opened the general store; Stillwell would have to make do without newspapers and milk.

Peter knew the answer. 'It's someone who hates humanity, someone who distrusts everyone else.'

'So what has that got to do with the painting?' asked Rex. 'Surely there's no suggestion that Revdev hates humanity?'

They'd studied the latest painting, as had half of Stillwell. It was only a little thing, a circular format no bigger than a dinner plate. So the artist had taped it to the inside of the tobacconist's window for easier viewing.

There were only two figures. Only one of them was recognisable, a perfect portrait of the Reverend Devon Batt. But the perfect portrait was set atop a small, hunched figure that was about to cut a money pouch from the belt of the second figure.

The second figure was puzzling, enigmatic. The figure in the book was tall but slightly stooped as though in quiet contemplation. It was cloaked entirely in black and with a cowl that all but obscured the face. The figure in the painting held the same pose but was robed in creamy white. A broad, purple sash draped across his shoulders. It was turned up to form a stiff collar which partly obscured the face. He wore a bishop's mitre and carried a bishop's crozier. It was obvious that the squat Revdev was stealing money from the bishop.

'According to this book,' Peter turned a page, 'Bruegel has depicted the misanthrope as the big, black figure. But the tobacconist's painting has replaced the misanthrope with a bishop. I reckon that the artist has used the Bruegel composition to tell us something. It really has nothing to do with misanthropy, it's more about…' He faltered.

Sally finished his explanation for him. 'It's all about theft, isn't it? This is about Revdev stealing from the bishop, from the church. That's it, isn't it? The bishop symbolises the whole church, doesn't he? The bastard artist is telling us that Revdev has been stealing from the church.' She turned to Peter. 'You're the church warden, Peter. Do you know anything about this?'

'No. Nothing.' Peter looked distraught. 'Nothing,' he repeated, and again, 'Nothing.' He drifted to the window and looked out at the most recent gathering of art critics next door. Then he turned to face his two fellow committee members. 'I don't believe it,' he said. 'That bloody painter has got it wrong this time. Devon's never stolen anything in his life. I'd bet my life on it.' His voice had become louder and more clipped than usual and his expression was one of near panic. It was almost as if it was he who was suffering a personal attack rather than the reverend.

'I agree,' nodded Rex. 'He's a decent bloke. What I don't understand is how the artist is able to pump out those paintings so quickly.'

'Like we said before, most of them must have been painted beforehand,' reminded Sally. 'This one could have been painted anytime.' She paused in thought. 'In fact, in fact…this painting might be referring to some incident in Revdev's life before he came to Stillwell.'

Peter was actually trembling as he spoke. 'I can't believe that. And…and even if there was something in his past, what would be the point of dragging it up now? What is that bastard in the tobacconist trying to prove? How far back in our past is he going to rummage, to slander us?' He moved back to the window. 'Look at those gawkers,' he spat. 'I bet that every one of them has a skeleton in their closet. How does this bastard know so much about everyone? Who's he going to crucify next?' He slumped into a chair, exhausted by his own outburst.

Sally and Rex glanced meaningfully at each other. Neither needed to delve very far into their pasts to find regrettable deeds. Some of Rex's real estate transactions had been mildly dodgy and some of his tax declarations belonged on the fiction shelves. Sally, by contrast, could have filled the fact shelves with some of her earlier exploits. The difference was that she took a certain pride in her nefarious activities. Any added notoriety that might come with exposure wouldn't worry her. In fact, it would probably enhance her reputation as a tough-nut publican.

But Peter? His reaction was quite extraordinary. He was really showing all the signs of panic.

Rex broke the introverted silence. 'Well, I suppose we'd better go and have a talk with Revdev. Don't know if he's seen the painting yet. Probably best if he gets the news from us.'

'No,' snapped Peter as he lurched out of his seat. 'I'll tell him. I'm the warden. Better that I talk to him.' Without another word, he stalked from the room.

Rex blew through puffed cheeks. 'Whew,' he breathed. 'Pete's really worked up. I suppose he's gotten pretty close to Revdev, so it's no wonder that he's defending him.'

Sally nodded. 'Tell you what I think, Rex. I reckon that our Peter has figured out that he's going to be next on the list.'

'You mean...'

'I mean that our Peter, our church warden, has got something in his past that he doesn't want to feature in the tobacconist's window.'

Rex considered this for a moment. 'You're right, Sal. That's why he's reacted so strongly to the Revdev painting. If the bastard artist is turning his attention to the church, then he'll probably have some dirt on Peter.' He flicked through several pages of the big *The Late Renaissance Outside of Italy* as if to find a clue. 'I wonder why he's only copied Bruegel's paintings. There's any number of other paintings that he might have copied.'

'Hadn't thought of that,' answered Sally. She pulled a chair closer to Rex so as to better study the book. 'What's so significant about Bruegel? What's it say about him?'

Rex started to read from the text. '"Bruegel, Pieter"... Hmmmm, "1520-something to 1569". Born in the Netherlands... Hmmm, so he's Dutch, thought to be... Oh shit, Sally, listen to this. "Place of birth uncertain but thought to be either Breda…or Brabant". Shit, Brabant, Sal, Brabant, Peter's surname. Bloody hell, Sal, that couldn't be a coincidence.'

'Shouldn't think so. Our bastard artist knows everything about everyone. That's why he's been copying Bruegel's pictures. Brabant is the common connection. And it's Pieter Bruegel – that's the same as Peter. Jeez, Rex, he's a clever bastard.'

'So we'd better tell Peter about this.'

'Yes, but let's take one problem at a time. Maybe we'll wait and see what's happening with Revdev first. Peter will probably be back sometime today to fill us in.

Sally was behind the front bar when Peter Brabant came in. There were a dozen drinkers arranged in groups of two or three along the bar. Two blokes were throwing darts without bothering to score.

The usual current affairs issues, sports scores and wheat prices had been relegated. Speculation about 'The Tobacconist' was now the topic of choice. Rumours of the school closure, the dwindling supplies of milk and the total absence of newspapers were affecting Stillwell at an idiosyncratic level. Few Stillwellians had been touched by the strange paintings that kept appearing in the tobacconist's window. Many had taken a smug, voyeuristic interest but hadn't, until now, appreciated the indirect consequences. The overdue comeuppance of a dodgy builder had been gossip-worthy for a day or two, but hardly momentous. On the other hand, they had been richly entertained by a bloke smacking a shop with a spade and further amused by the little tête-à-tête between their Amazonian publican and the pompous copper. These were welcome distractions to be enjoyed from a distance, but not having enough milk to pour on your Weetbix, well, that was different, that was a personal inconvenience. The general consensus was that someone should do something about it.

Peter was obviously shaken. He made for the quiet end of the bar, away from the drinkers, and beckoned to Sally to join him.

She brought a beer with her and pushed it across the bar to Peter. 'What's happened, mate? How's the rev?'

The warden took a long pull at his beer and half-emptied the glass. 'He's buggered, Sal.'

'How do mean, buggered?'

'Stuffed, shattered. He was a blubbering mess, been hitting the Scotch a bit hard too, '

'So he'd seen the painting?'

'No,' he drained the glass. 'That's the weird thing. He hasn't even seen the bloody painting. He got a registered letter this morning from the diocese. He has to attend an enquiry next week to answer questions about the embezzlement of funds from his last parish.'

'Hell,' Sal took his glass and returned with a fresh beer. It gave her time to surmise. 'It's too much of a coincidence to expect that the painting and the registered letter arrived at the same time by chance. Our bastard painter had this all set up long ago.'

'Yes,' answered the warden. 'The worst part is that Revdev is guilty, Sal. He told me…he told me about ripping off the church accounts at his last parish in the city. Some kind of building fund that he had responsibility for.'

'Bloody hell. Did he say how much?'

'No. He was in too much of a mess and I didn't want to press him for details.'

Sally moved away to serve several thirsty customers. She rarely drank when she was behind the bar but, when she returned, she brought another beer for Peter and a double brandy and dry for herself. She was careful with her words, cautioned by the unsettling thought that Peter was likely to be high on the painter's hit list. 'One problem at a time,' she advised herself.

'So, what's the rev going to do?'

'From what I can gather, he's going to front up to the diocese enquiry and confess everything. He hadn't told his wife yet, Sal. She knows that something is up but she hasn't got a clue what it is, Christ! What a bloody mess.'

The publican took a sip of her brandy. 'Might be a good idea if you was to go back and check up on them, Peter. It'd be awful if he went and did something stupid. I mean, something really stupid. Especially if he's hitting the bottle. At the very least you might be able to help his missus get through this.'

Peter hung his head and sighed. 'Yes, you're right. I'd better go back and see what I can do.' He pushed his half-full glass away and swivelled off the bar stool.

Sally had never seen the normally robust warden look so deflated, so impotent. He barely acknowledged Rex as they passed in the doorway and he headed into the night.

That night *The Misanthrope* was removed from the window. It had, like *The Peasant Dance* and *The Land of Cockaigne*, hung for just one day. That was as long as it needed.

The tobacconist's window remained empty for four days. There was no church service on Sunday; Revdev had packed up and left Stillwell. His wife went with him but, according to Peter Brabant, she was spitting venom and almost incandescent with anger. The diocese decided that the church would remain closed until Christmas, when the clergyman from Osmond would conduct the traditional service. Until then, worshippers must travel to Osmond each Sunday to attend services.

The school remained closed. Bert Lister, the school council chairman, reported that the regional office was having trouble finding an available teacher at this late stage of the year. If one couldn't be found by the end of the week, then the kids would have to be bussed to Osmond for the remainder of the year. The regional director had not been very subtle in suggesting that the bussing, once begun, would probably become permanent and Stillwell's school would close permanently.

Quentin Ball reopened the general store on Saturday. Most of the other High Street traders had pitched in. Kath Lister from the bakery; Lawrence Johns's wife, Silva, from the butchers; Maurice Harris from the pharmacy; and Rex Reynolds spent most of Friday getting the place in order. They weren't particularly forgiving of Cuey's infidelity but their own businesses were suffering. With the closing of the general store, many locals found it necessary to travel to Osmond for essentials like milk and vegies. While they were in Osmond they found it convenient to also shop for their meat, and bread and pharmaceuticals. No one doubted that, if the Stillwell general store remained closed, all of the other High Street businesses would collapse.

The hairdresser stayed closed and rumour had it that Sharyn Foxwell had joined the exodus from Stillwell.

Not all of the news was depressing. Stillwell's cricketers had extended their purple patch by bowling out Anfield for 69 in just twenty-five overs. At stumps on Saturday, they were sitting on 48 for the loss of 1 wicket.

Lawrence Johns was called upon to deliver another carton of schnitzels to the pub where Sally was flat out catering to both the cricketers and the victorious women's tennis team which had creamed the ladies from Anfield.

So you couldn't get your hair cut in Stillwell, and you couldn't get a chook shed built and you couldn't go to church. And your kids couldn't go to school.

But Ulysses himself had observed that 'The heavens themselves observe priority and place and custom.' So priority and custom dictated that you could still play cricket and tennis on Saturdays and, on Tuesday nights, you could still play darts.

Churchies were to play Pub Blue and there had been some hopeful speculations that the God-botherers might be forced to forfeit, given that their number three player, Revdev, had done a bunk.

Churchies captain Peter Brabant was in no mood for darts but, equally, not in the mood to countenance the ignominious forfeiture of a match. At the last moment, he elevated the team's fourth player into third spot and press-ganged the husband of the church organist to fill the vacancy. Heroic sporting conventions demanded that this would become an audacious encounter with the new, untried but plucky recruit jagging the winning dart in a nail-biting climax. Such was not to be the case, as he managed to hit the wall more often than he hit the dartboard. Churchies went down for the first time in a long time.

Inspired by the Pub Blues' victory, arch-rivals but brothers- in-venue, Pub Red, lifted their game and scraped home over second-placed Cockies. This was reason enough for both pub teams to shout an extra round of beers which, as custom demanded, had to be acknowledged and matched by the losing teams by buying an extra congratulatory round. So, for the second time in the past few days, Ulysses' maxim on priorities came into play and everybody got mildly, and happily, plastered.

Fortunately, Senior Cont-stable Garth Staker was not on hand to witness the illegal flaunting of hotel trading hours nor the rather disorderly departure of two dozen sportsmen. In one way this was unfortunate for, had he been lurking in the vicinity of Howarth's Railway Hotel, he might have witnessed the installation of a new painting in the tobacconist's window.

The Late Renaissance Outside of Italy described Bruegel's painting of *Parable of the Blind* as 'confronting, both in composition and subject'. It depicts a procession of six blind, disfigured men. Each is leading the other by means of a wooden staff. They are arranged in awkward, uncoordinated poses. The leader of the group has fallen into a ditch and the rest, being linked by their staffs, seem certain to follow. The composition, the line of blind men, is a diagonal. The last of the group stands in the top left corner, the fallen figure is in the bottom right. The landscape behind them is dominated by a church.

The painting in the tobacconist's window was faithful to the original in all but three details, but they were very significant details. The church had been altered to clearly represent Stillwell's St Margaret's C of E. Five of the blind men were dressed in baggy, pale grey prison garb each bearing a distinct yellow Star of David. The sixth man, standing erect and arrogantly in the top left corner was neither blind nor disfigured. Rather than being part of the ragged and desperate procession, this evil-looking man was obviously driving the others forward. He held an officer's riding crop with which he jabbed the sightless and miserable creature in front of him. His uniform was that of a Nazi SS *Oberführer* with the distinctive crimson armbands bearing swastikas. He was, unmistakably, Peter Brabant.

Peter never saw the painting. He was shaken awake by his wife on Wednesday morning and it took a little while for her urgent exhortations to penetrate his mild hangover. There were men at the door – four men, two in suits and two in police uniforms – demanding that they speak with Peter. The two in suits had identified themselves as federal police. They had been contacted by an anonymous caller before the *Parable of the Blind* had appeared in the window. Just as the diocese knew all about Revdev before *The Misanthrope* had appeared.

The rest of Stillwell saw the painting. It was large, it was grotesque, and no one doubted for a minute that it was true. The tobacconist painter had the firmly established credentials of one who knew the truth. Wally Dunn had been proven to be a thief, Janette Wilson had been proven to be an addict, Quentin Ball had been proven to be a philanderer and Sharyn Foxwell a tart, Devon Batt had been proven to be a larcenist. Who could doubt that Peter Brabant was a Nazi, a war criminal?

So the crowd gathered under the tobacconist's veranda to gawk at this most damning of paintings. They nodded sagely and they clicked their tongues. Some declared their long-held but unspoken suspicions about Peter, the clipped voice, the faint accent that he claimed to be South African, or was it Dutch? Anyone could tell that it was really German. And he always wanted to take charge of things. Bloody typical. Bloody good at throwing darts...well, that srood to reason, didn't it?

It wasn't until after the pub closed and the town fell into silent darkness that the last of the experts dispersed and went home.

The fire siren went off at three in the morning. It took twelve minutes for the small band of volunteer fire-fighters to arrive with Stillwell's inadequate fire truck, by which time the tobacconist's was fully engulfed and the paint on both the pub and the general store was starting to blister. The crowd that had so recently passed opinion on the artworks now rallied to form makeshift bucket brigades in the laneway behind the buildings.

It took a further fifteen minutes for the larger fire unit to arrive from Osmond. They were able to prevent the blaze from spreading to the neighbouring pub and store but the entire roof of the tobacconist's had collapsed into the inferno and the building was reduced to four sandstone walls that also threatened to disintegrate.

The dawn was grey with a light drizzle. A few charred timbers, still harbouring remnant embers, hissed and crackled until no heat remained. The stench of smoke hung over the High Street as Senior Cont-stable Garth Staker and Errol 'Wet-behind-the-ears' Clements strung yellow and black striped plastic tape around what had once been a tobacconist shop but was now nothing more than a danger to the public.

They'd made a quick reconnoitre of the interior, always conscious of the threat presented by the weakened sandstone walls. The destruction was complete. You'd never know that anyone had ever lived in there.

By nine o'clock, the Osmond school bus had picked up the kids and the shops had opened for business. The few people on the High Street looked apprehensively to the sky. The drizzle was turning to rain and a wall of purple-black clouds was massing on the western horizon. With the wheat crop so close to harvest, the last thing they wanted was a thunderstorm.

Ronnie Smalls

1962

There were 'Welcome to Hughburton. Pop 485' signs at each end of the High Street. If you missed them, you'd be hard-pressed to pick Hughburton from any number of other mallee towns.

There used to be a lot more towns, in lines across the mallee, each separated from the next by a day's ride in a Cobb & Co. coach. The railway spelt the death of both Cobb & Co. and many of the settlements, reduced them to little more than a couple of grain silos, a handful of fibro fettler's houses and a scattering of limestone chimneys standing like memorials to the houses that were plundered for their timbers and corrugated iron years ago.

Hughburton survived. Not through the gritty determination or the bustling industry of its townsfolk but because it straddled Mosquito Creek, the only permanent water for miles. Steam trains needed water, so Hughburton survived. It was, like most smallish communities, a bit of a fish bowl, albeit dusty. Everyone knew everyone else's personal business whether or not they wanted their personal business known.

So everyone knew that Ronnie's dad was the idiot who stole the railway station clock.

It was a simple clock. Big black numerals displayed on a plain white face. It was mounted in a modest little weatherboard tower topped by a cockerel vane that had jammed facing north, so it was right most of the time. An encircling strip of understated cast-iron filigree contrasted nicely with the corrugated iron steeple. The tower stood atop the neat red-brick station building with the snug, one-bedroom stationmaster's residence.

The clock faced onto Railway Terrace and could be clearly seen from the High Street, one of those things that everyone took for granted and never really noticed except when they checked their watches against it.

That they could check their watches with confidence was due to the stationmaster, Mr Thomas, who was a prim and particular gentleman in all his dealings. He diligently and daily ascended the narrow internal ladder within the modest little tower, where there was just room enough to reach up and rewind the clockwork.

This task was completed by 7.32 each morning, after which he swept the station platform then watered the eight hare's-foot ferns that hung in baskets from the eaves and the sixteen potted geraniums precisely spaced around the building. The watering can would be returned to its rightful place beneath the rainwater tank and the broom hung behind the entrance door just as the clock's metallic chime reminded Hughburton that it was now eight o'clock.

Mr Thomas's morning routine was a comforting constant which reflected the way that the good folk of Hughburton liked things done.

Ronnie's dad was an incongruity. For starters, he didn't have a steady job. He was usually busy but it was mostly fixing fences, digging septics and the like. Odd jobs, nothing regular. He had an old Studebaker ute…well, more of a chopped-off buckboard really; got it in exchange for some fencing work. Hard to say who got the better part of that deal. He'd painted 'Jack Smalls. No job too Small' on the doors but the gearbox had seized so it never left his backyard.

Jack Smalls was known around Hughburton as 'Hydraulic Jack'. It was a nickname that, when explained, pointed to a darker side of the man. Because Jack Smalls, like his nickname, would lift anything.

Things went missing when Hydraulic Jack was around. If you hired him to do a spot of gardening, you needed to count the wheels on your wheelbarrow before you paid him. Or, as the blokes in the pub would advise, 'Count your fingers after you shake his hand.'

So Jack rarely got any indoor work. The publican couldn't trust

Jack anywhere near the bottle shop. The butcher found himself forever counting his sausages and the baker tallying his lamingtons if Jack was on the job.

The thing about Jack was that he was a really likeable bloke. He was gentle and quietly spoken and always willing to pitch in on community projects and fund-raising barbecues. All you had to do was go around to his place and fetch back the tongs that he'd nicked during the day.

Hydraulic Jack was, in short, a pleasant kleptomaniac. So the town made allowances. The kids didn't tease Ronnie about his dad and the Hughburton womenfolk welcomed his mum, Melody, into their clubs and organisations such as the Agricultural and Horticultural Society and the Tidy Towns Committee. And Melody's standing in Hughburton was certainly enhanced by the fact that she was the only seamstress and dressmaker in town, and she was really good at it.

It is also fair to say that the Smalls were not alone in the open secret club. There were many who couldn't afford to throw stones from within their own glasshouses. Darren Maker's mum, for example, had an extraordinary collection of fur coats in her wardrobe and every time she visited the Big Smoke for a weekend she came back with another. And it was amazing how many blokes needed to visit the barber, after hours, on Tuesdays, the same evening that the greyhounds were running in the Big Smoke. Tony McCann was one such regular client, an unlikely client for a barber, being that Tony was as bald as a five-watt light bulb, and half as bright.

The local copper, Dave Watson, rejoiced in the sobriquet of 'Doc' in honour of Doctor Watson, Sherlock's offsider. He'd been coppering for more years than a politician has evasions. He'd grown up in a country community much like Hughburton but had spent most of his time in uniform pounding the bloodied and booze-soaked pavements of the Big Smoke. It left him with an understanding of human frailties and corruptions that would have Freud lying in a foetal ball under his own couch. He'd reported on enough knifings, beatings and bastard acts to fill a room full of scriptwriters and had come to yearn for a quieter beat. Hughburton suited him like a bow-tie suits a penguin.

It became Doc's routine to stroll around the town as it woke in the morning and, again, after it had settled in for the evening. He liked the calm hustle of the awakening High Street: shopkeepers setting up trestles of half-priced specials in denial of council by-laws, kids walking to school and half-heartedly telling their faithful dogs to go home.

In the evenings, he might hear disjointed snatches of radio programs from behind drawn curtains. Occasionally he'd sympathise with kids struggling through piano practice. On hot summer evenings, neighbours might gather on front verandas for a beer or a cup of tea. The shadow of the local copper strolling past became a familiar comfort.

Country coppering required an understanding of both community dynamics and pragmatic justice. The letter of the law didn't always sit well, unless it was a manifestly serious offence like murder, violence or sheep-stealing.

Doc understood that it wasn't in anyone's interest, for example, to gaol a minor offender if he was meant to be opening the batting for Hughburton next day. And slapping a fine on a bloke for illegal parking could prove to be awkward if he turned out to be your partner in Sunday's bowls doubles.

So Doc had become adept at surreptitiously taking an offender around the corner for a quiet verbal kick in the backside along with the gentle suggestion that, next time, it might not be verbal.

Trouble was, the copper had taken Hydraulic Jack around the corner once too often and his admirable patience, along with the townsfolks' tolerance, was starting to wear a bit thin.

Doc was first to notice the missing clock when he'd stepped out for his customary evening stroll around Hughburton. It was just on half-past nine, so the town was in darkness. A few lights glinted through lace curtains and he could hear snippets of an ABC concert broadcast. A lone dog barked at nothing and got nothing in return.

As usual, Doc checked his watch against the...against the large, round hole in the railway station tower. Then he noticed a ladder propped against the tower. Then he noticed a shadowy figure stagger off under the weight of a large, round object.

The copper followed at a discreet distance. No need to get closer; he knew who it was that was staggering under the weight of the large, round object, and he knew where he lived. Besides, Jack's laboured breathing could have been heard by a deaf donkey in a diver's helmet.

As expected, Jack turned into his gate and staggered down to his garden shed. It was there that the copper caught up with him.

'Evening, Jack.'

Hydraulic Jack nearly jumped out of his stolen boots. 'Gawd, Doc,' he stammered. 'Y' nearly gave me a corollary.'

'That'd be a coronary, Jack,' advised the copper and then added, 'Been doing a spot of night-time clock maintenance, have we?'

'Don't know what you mean, D...' stuttered Jack as the station clock struck ten from the garden shed.

Hughburton boasted pretty much one of everything; one pub, one butcher, one baker, one general store, one stock agent, one barber, one policeman, one stationmaster, one postman, one council clerk, one school teacher and one dressmaker.

There is, in the mallee, a long-standing tradition that farms are handed down from parents to their offspring. In Hughburton, it was not only farms that passed from father to son: most of the businesses and trades also passed from one generation to the next.

The publican, for example, had taken over from his father, who had inherited it from his own father. The baker was second-generation and the butcher's grandfather had started selling chops sixty years earlier. Even the youngish postman had inherited his father's canvas shoulder bag after last year's tragic incident with the rogue ram. The council clerk, Mavis Grassroots, was training her young Felicity in anticipation of the day when she could hand over the ledgers and pursue her dream of writing romantic novellas.

So all of Ronnie's classmates had their futures secured; they all expected to take over the family farm, or shop, or whatever it was that their parents did to bring home the bacon. This left Ronnie in a bit of a pickle: what to do when he left school? His dad was in the clink so if he left Hughburton his mum would be all alone. But then she barely earned enough with her dressmaking business, so he'd have to find some way of helping the family budget. After a lot of tortuous thought, Ronnie decided to stick with local tradition and follow in his father's footsteps – not as an odd-job man, no: Ronnie would become Hughburton's one and only criminal.

He knew that his dad wasn't a terribly effective criminal. A yardstick of his success could be seen in his inches-thick record of arrests. But he also knew that his dad's shortfalls had nothing to do with him not being the brightest candle on the cake; no, Jack was a fairly intelligent bloke. But compulsive kleptomania doesn't consider consequences.

Young Ronnie wasn't a kleptomaniac. In fact, he rarely acted on compulsion. Rather, he was obsessed with intricate planning. He revelled in minutiae, in details. When he assembled a plastic biplane construction kit, he actually followed the instructions with the correct sequence of assembly. He sandpapered the rough bits and painted each component before sticking them together. He put the little model pilot in place before he stuck on the top wing.

Planning and preparation, that was the key to successful crime. No problems. Ronnie could make Hannibal's crossing look like a stroll to the letter box. And research: he needed to research. No problems. Ronnie was well-known at the library. Particularly at the end of the month when the overdue notices were mailed out.

He was an avid but very slow reader of paperback crime novels, which he fastidiously dissected – not just the plot but every phrase and every sentence. This meant that he hardly ever finished a book before he received the library's overdue slip. So he usually read the first half where the crime is committed but rarely the second half which described the forensic investigation, the arrest and the punishment. It usually transpires, in the concluding paperback chapters, that the criminal mastermind has overlooked something, something like the dirty smudge of contaminating pollen from a plant that blooms for just five hours and within a security zone so restricted that only one bloke has clearance to enter it. Or the single hair from his balaclava that can be traced back to the actual sheep that produced the hair and hence to the boutique balaclava shop where the owner can recall the address, phone number and description of every customer that has walked through the door since the shop opened four years ago.

Or the single biggest mistake that gets 'em every time: the telephone. Because the phone company, which in reality likely has a list of customers' complaints as long as your arm, can, in its fictional version, provide records of every phone call made in the past decade, and from whom, and to whom, and probably their addresses, and possibly their descriptions.

But all of this was unknown to Ronnie, who hardly ever got to those chapters in the books.

One thing that he learned from his reading was that he needed a title, an epithet. The standard Hughburton titles like postman or grocer were obvious, but what did a resident criminal call himself? He sought inspiration from his paperbacks; 'Gangster' sounded good but 'was inappropriate for a solo criminal and Cat Burglar' brought on his allergy. 'The Slasher' didn't fit with his intended criminal activities nor did 'The Scarlet Lady'.

Then he remembered that the criminal mastermind in *Elliot Spade Cracks the Case* was a devilishly clever character called the 'Will-o'-the-wisp' who could insert himself, or herself, into the tightest situations, steal whatever took his, or her, fancy and then leave a cryptic clue to confuse the dicks. This was right up Ronnie's alley: meticulous planning, cunning execution and a wraith-like escape that left the flat-foots…well, flat-footed.

He could abbreviate Will-o'-the-Wisp to Wow, which would look terrific on calling cards and as a headline on the *Hughburton Highlights*. Well, OK, the *Hughburton Highlights* was only a single-page newsletter published by Mavis Grassroots and half of it was given over to serialised versions of her romantic novellas. But a headline like 'Wow strikes again' would always trump 'Gladys Newberry wins Best Lillypilly Jam'.

So the Will-o'-the-wisp, Wow, began planning his new career. He began, where all good crims began, by casing the joint. This involved determining the best avenues of ingress and egress, which basically meant getting in and out, but sounded more copperish.

In the evenings, to the whirring accompaniment of his mum's sewing machine and as moth squadrons attacked the screen door, he would lie on the cool lino floor and make exquisitely detailed maps and drawings. Sometimes he made business cards to leave at the scenes of his criminal triumphs. He found a beaut cartoon of a vampire wearing a plumed hat and swirling his cloak across his face so that only one malevolent eye could be seen. It made a really good Will-o'-the-wisp if he left the plume out of the hat. He painstakingly copied the cartoon onto pieces of card cut from cereal boxes and added WOW in capitals. Pictures of cornflakes on the reverse were unfortunate, but possibly cryptic.

After several reconnoitres of possible targets, Ronnie – sorry, Wow – decided that his first target would be the general store. It was loaded with nickable items. The owners, Mr and Mrs Cole, lived with their two daughters above the store. Wow was certain that he could execute a silent ingress and egress without alerting the family. It was in his favour that the daughters liked kittens and didn't have a dog.

In his mind's eye, he could see Mr Cole descending the stairs to find his shelves empty but for the single, cryptic business card. This was the sort of boldly romantic imagery that sold paperbacks.

On further thought, he realised that, to leave the shelves empty, he'd need to shift about eight tons of canned beans and boxed biscuits. No problems: he'd covertly visit the store during open hours and identify which selective items would make the best booty, things that were easiest to carry away and easiest to fence. Another note to himself: he'd need to find a fence sometime.

He raided his Dan Dare pressed-tin spaceship money box and, working on the premise that you had to spend money to make money, visited the store four times a day to purchase a single halfpenny sherbet bomb. Each visit took fifteen minutes of surreptitious scrutiny of the shelves and furtive jottings in his notebook before he stepped boldly to the counter and bought the pink lolly.

By the seventh visit on the second day, Ronnie – sorry, Wow – had convinced himself that he was a near-undetectable will-o'-the-wisp. Mr Cole, however, had twigged that something was up after his second visit on the first day. The grocer had his suspicions confirmed when he spotted Ronnie measuring the side window using a wooden school ruler that he had secreted in his sock. It had made him walk oddly when he'd left with his sixth sherbet bomb just an hour earlier.

Mr Cole was another of Hughburton's genial citizens. He made a comfortable living from the inherited Cole's Emporium and always donated items to fund-raising raffles. Cole's Emporium always got a sponsor's mention in the *Hughburton Highlights*. It didn't give Mr Cole a competitive edge, because there wasn't any competition, but he did it anyway.

Cole's Emporium didn't have a security system, not even a dog. In fact, in summer the windows were left open to catch the evening breezes. Security around Hughburton had been even more relaxed, if that were possible, since the town's only criminal had been put behind bars.

Everyone in Hughburton sympathised with Melody and Ronnie Smalls. Mrs Cole had several of Melody's creations in her wardrobe and her daughters had been friends with young Ronnie at school. Mr Cole was reluctant to act on Ronnie's strange behaviour but it was only too obvious that the lad was planning a heist. He'd go and have a quiet word with Doc Watson.

The storekeeper was not alone in his suspicions. Ronnie's mum was having a few doubts about her son's evening activities. He'd always been diligent with his homework but scholastic pursuits during school holidays were sort of sinister. His cricket gear had hardly come out of his wardrobe and his tennis racket was gathering dust on top.

His usual holiday routine was to race off after wolfing down his breakfast and then return later with mud up to his armpits, a dozen yabbies in a bucket and a couple of mates looking for cheese and sauce sandwiches to eat in the tree house. But Ronnie had taken to slinking home in much the same cleanish condition in which he'd left and then furtively retiring to his bedroom for hours.

Mothers of lads have plenty to worry about. Melody had more concerns than a mermaid in a minefield. She was torn between her fervent desire to trust her son and the fervent desire to know what the little devil was up to, so she snuck into his bedroom. She didn't know what she expected to find or what she wanted to find. Or, rather, what she didn't want to find. Nearly-teenage boys present a lot of possibilities.

The little pile of sherbet bomb wrappers on his bedside table next to his Dan Dare money box was unexpected but not particularly worrying. There was a paperback; *Elliot Spade Cracks the Case*. She sat on his bed and flipped through it. Her heels kicked something under the bed and she reached down to find a cardboard box full of mysteries; a stack of cards with a strange cartoon and Wow written on one side and cornflakes on the other, possibly cryptic.

She found an odd list: pocket knives, fishing gear, fountain pens, bike lights, batteries, model planes, microscope, chewing gum, choc and comics. Dozens of disparate items each with a number and a letter pencilled alongside. Chewing gum was C1, choc was C2, fountain pens were E3 and comics were E6. Some sort of identifying code?

The sketches of Cole's Emporium were very precise. The attention to detail was commendable: every shelf was pencilled in, as were the dimensions of the side window. And then she noticed that there were little numbers and letters identifying specific places on the store's shelves.

The same identifying codes that were on the list. The list of items that you might find on the shelves in…a general store. Oh, my heavens!

She took a last look and then, reluctantly, put everything back in its place and pulled Ronnie's bedroom door closed behind her. She barely made it back to the kitchen before her son came in through the back screen door.

'Hi, Ronnie,' she said in a voice about three times too high and through a smile about three times too wide. 'What have you been up to?' And then, because the question sounded too inquisitional, she hastily added, 'Would you like some lunch? I've got some canned spag in tomato sauce.'

'Good oh, Mum,' he answered in a voice that she thought might be just a tad too casual. 'Back in a minute.' He disappeared down the passage and into his room. Perhaps just a little too quickly? And was that a school ruler sticking out of his sock?

What to do? To confront Ronnie would be to reveal the bedroom search. To ignore the evidence could see him joining dad in the clink. After lunch she'd go and have a quiet word with Doc Watson.

Having a quiet word with both a potential victim and a potential thief's mum, and both within ten minutes of each other was a novelty for Doc. Back in the Big Smoke he'd have probably got abused by one and knifed by the other. But here in Hughburton…well, you didn't often to get the opportunity to solve a crime before it happened.

Time for another quiet word around the corner.

No one will ever know what the policeman said to the would-be thief. Dave Watson never revealed what transpired during his quiet words around the corner. None of his interviewees ever divulged what the big copper had to say; keeping schtumm was part of the deal. So the encouraging words, or threats, or advice that passed in confidence between him and Wow – sorry, between him and Ronnie – have remained confidential.

Mr Cole witnessed the dramatic moment when Doc stepped out from behind the magazine rack and collared young Ronnie as he was measuring the distance between pocket knives (P1) and the window. He was on hands and knees as he end-over-ended his school ruler, not a good position for a quick getaway

The lad's feet touched the ground twice as Doc took him out of the shop and around the corner for a quiet word. He was assisted by the copper's huge hand under his armpit, his shoulder just one click away from dislocation.

It was one of the longest quiet words ever visited on a suspect by Doc. Mr Cole counted a good fifteen minutes before the pair emerged from around the corner. This time, the policeman's hand was gentle on the lad's shoulder.

Ronnie's face was red and moist. His right sleeve looked to have reached saturation point and the left was being called into play. There was a final conversation outside the store…well, not so much a conversation as a final quiet word from Doc and a lot of damp nodding from the lad with further applications of the left sleeve.

Finally, the copper grasped the lad by both shoulders, turned him homeward and gave him a gentle but persuasive shove. Ronnie sloped off across the road with shoulders slumping, head hanging low, heels dragging, lip drooping and with his tail between his legs.

'Might be a future for the boy as a contortionist,' thought Doc as he watched the twisted figure depart. He turned back to the emporium, gave Mr Cole a thumbs-up through the window and strolled off with another victory for country justice under his belt.

Melody was at her sewing machine when her son crept through the screen door. She pretended not to notice him, bent lower over the fabric and pressed her foot firmly on the pedal until the machine fairly screamed. She managed to sew fifty yards of random zigzag until she was certain that he'd got to his bedroom. Later it would take her about four hours to unpick it.

She was in the kitchen beating a cake mix when Ronnie came down the passage carrying the cardboard box from under his bed. He had to pass through the kitchen to get to the back door, so she bent lower over the bowl, turned the beater to its maximum setting and busied herself with cracking eggs into the mix. By the time he reached the backyard, she'd added a dozen eggs and the beater had circulated a horizontal line of batter across her midriff and around the kitchen. Later it would take her an hour to scrape it off.

Her son slowly emptied the cardboard box into the old forty-four-gallon drum that they used as an incinerator. There was a will-o'-the-wisp of smoke as he put a match to his painstakingly prepared plans.

It may just have been a stray drop of cake batter that got into her eye and had her reaching for her hanky.

1970

There is a small crowd gathered. Melody is there, as is Doc and all of the Coles. In fact, half of Hughburton has made the rare train trip to the Big Smoke.

Jack Small stands proudly beside his wife, proud of his family, proud of the fact that he's now free of the kleptomaniac monkey that's been riding on his back for so many years. Proud of the HR Holden ute parked in the yard back in Hughburton with 'Jack Smalls. No Job Too Small' painted on the doors. He's had his business logo printed on cards; it's a hydraulic jack – part of the therapy.

Everyone's drinking champagne and nibbling little puff pastries filled with creamed chicken and mushrooms – you'd need about fifty to make a meal.

A svelte little jazz trio is oozing music into cracks in the conversation.

The setting is the opening of a chic little boutique in a trendy district studded with chic little boutiques. What sets this chic little boutique apart from the others is the name picked out in bold, gold script on the non-functional but chic awning over the ingress: RONNY.

There's a large gaggle of fashion journalists concentrating on each other. They are all leggy, frosty, lip-curly types who have seen a hundred of these awfully young and terribly eager designers come and go. They are only here for the free champagne and vol-au-vents and to scribble a few brief notes which they'll later use in acidic columns full of cruel adjectives like 'hackneyed', or 'passé', or '*démodé*'.

But then one of them, champagne-charged and high-heeled, accidentally stumbles against a mannequin and, as she gracelessly slides downwards, can't help but notice the fine cut, the intricate workmanship and the exquisite attention to detail. She is not so sozzled and jaundiced as to be unimpressed. She regains her poise by climbing back up the mannequin and, with the support of this new best friend, studies some of the other garments on display.

Hang on! This is different! This stuff is a cut above the average. Get it? A cut above the average? He, he, he. Ooops, sorry. Wonder who this RONNY character is? Check out the label… Hmm. WOW, that's not a bad name for a fashion range. This might be worth a decent review, been a while since I wrote one of those. Where's my bloody pen? Where's my bloody glass?

Her colleagues are each closely monitoring the others, their vixen-radars humming. They notice that she has noticed something that they haven't. My God! Was she actually taking notes? Was there something different about RONNY? Better take a closer look… Amazing, this gear isn't too bad, nice workmanship, got a touch of quality about it. Hmm, might have to submit a decent review. Where's my bloody pen?

A Hughburton tradition has continued. Aanother trade has passed from one generation to the next.

Ronny – sorry, RONNY – gives his mum a hug.

The Turk

Lance Corporal 'Winkie' Williams shifted position slightly to relieve the ache in his lower back. Lying up here on this sandstone ridge was playing merry hell with his injuries. The wounds to his hip and thigh meant that he couldn't put any pressure on his left side. It was difficult to keep motionless for more than a few minutes. The more he thought about it, the more painful it got.

Still, this was a bloody good vantage point. He had a clear sight down the barrel of his .303 to where he'd figured the Turk would appear. It might be a bit uncomfortable but he was determined to stay here for as long as it took, as long as it took to put a bullet into that bloody Turk.

He'd crawled up here under cover of the pre-dawn darkness, while the ground was still damp with dew. No chance of the Turk appearing before daylight, so he'd ignored the discomfort and quietly shifted a few rocks to clear a lying space and to build a bit of a low parapet, a castellation. He'd be invisible to anyone down below.

With his preparations complete, Corporal Williams had let his mind wander, recalling the events that had led to this cold and damp sandstone ridge, right back to the family farm just out of Ruby Hill.

Events in Europe didn't count for much in Ruby Hill. By the time the news had travelled from England to Sydney then out to Gunnedah and then up to Ruby Hill, it was days old and hardly worth worrying about.

News that the Australian government had pledged twenty thousand Aussie soldiers to help the Poms lick the Huns stirred a bit of interest. No one in Ruby Hill had any idea whether Australia had twenty thousand soldiers. It sounded like a lot. Might need to call for some volunteers to make up the numbers – probably be plenty of slackers in the Big Smoke could sign up. Wouldn't be a bad lurk, though, sign up for a few months, get a boat ride to England, see a bit of the world and get paid to do it. Yer.

But then a couple of blokes from up the track at Narrabri had got wind of the recruitment marches. God only knows how they found out about them but they sounded like a good lark, so they decided to start one of their own, to march from Narrabri to Tamworth. They'd convinced a few mates to join them, young blokes keen for a bit of an adventure. Then a couple of older blokes, in their thirties or forties and veterans of the Boer War, had offered to come along too. No one knew where these older blokes had come from; they just turned up in the pub at about the same time as news of the recruitment marches reached Narrabri. Good fellows they were, always ready to stand a beer for a young bloke and tell yarns about the Boer War.

The older blokes made a big difference; they knew all about the romance of soldiering overseas. They'd tasted real fighting, the thrill of armed combat. Mostly they played down the danger and jabbered on about the mateship, the excitement, the loyalty and the patriotism.

Whenever their group reached a town, like Turrawan or Boggabri, it was these older blokes who stirred up the locals with glamorous stories of our fighting men, protecting our commonwealth, protecting our wives and kids and sweethearts, how the brave English soldiers were facing enormous odds and needed us Aussies to come to their aid. Think of it, lads, good military training, overseas travel, smack those bastard Huns and come home a hero. And getting paid all along the way! Go home and pack a bedroll, lads, join the fun, join the volunteers, join the march.

By the time they got to Ruby Hill, they'd numbered forty-two. By the time they left Ruby Hill, they'd numbered forty-five. Len 'Winkie' Williams had joined them, as had Tom Chapel and Martin Jones. The few young men who hadn't signed up weren't to be seen when the march moved on; they'd slunk off somewhere.

There was a big turn-out when they reached Gunnedah. News of their recruitment march had preceded them and there was quite a crowd gathered in front of the Imperial Hotel, which had been, appropriately, Breaker Morant's watering hole. It gave the two Boer War veterans an ideal prelude to their rousing exhortations. It worked as it was meant to: sixteen young blokes joined the march as it left Gunnedah for the final forty-eight miles to Tamworth.

There was a big AIF tent pitched on the banks of the Peel River in Tamworth. It had to be big – eighty-four marchers followed the two old hands inside to where recruitment officers sat behind trestles and four doctors ushered each young man into a screened-off cubicle for a medical inspection. All but thirteen passed the doctors' scrutiny; six of them were sent packing because they had crook teeth. All thirteen were shepherded outside and left to find their own way back home.

The sky was lightening, but not by much. He'd seen a few stars while he was creeping up to here, up to the ridge. Now it looked like a blanket of blueish-grey cloud had snuck in with him. The sun was nothing more than a blur of pale light, like the light of a lantern diffused through the walls of a tent. It was still damp and chilly and it didn't look like the day was going get much warmer. Never mind. With luck, the Turk would show himself soon and then Winkie could do what had to be done and get away from here.

He checked his .303 for the umpteenth time and settled back down to wait. He had plenty of time.

He'd been to Kensington racecourse a couple of times, when his family made one of their rare and epic trips to the Big Smoke. Dad enjoyed a bit of a punt but always complained that the infrequent race meetings at Tamworth and Gunnedah didn't offer many opportunities to make a decent quid. Truth be known, Dad rarely made a decent quid at Kensington, but he never lost much either and the family enjoyed poring over the form guide and laying threepenny wagers on those neddies with the most impressive-sounding names.

But Kensington hadn't seen a racehorse for a while; it was almost unrecognisable as a race track. The grassed swath in the middle was covered by a sprawling maze of tents and a few temporary wooden barrack buildings. Off to one side was a sandy parade ground and an obstacle course. The famous home straight had become a rifle range, with targets arranged against a big earthen embankment that now bulged across the finish line that horses once raced towards. There were horses, Walers mostly, hundreds of them stabled and paddocked where their thoroughbred cousins used to be pampered.

It was here that he and his seventy recruited mates from the hinterland joined hundreds of others from all over rural New South Wales. Most of them had also been swept up by recruitment marches – they called them the Cooee marches. Some apparently random decisions made by some unknown officers saw the mob divided into units of infantry, artillery or cavalry. It didn't make much difference to the training; they all spent endless hours on the parade ground deciding which was their left foot and which was their right. They received instruction on how to salute and who you were supposed to salute at. This was particularly awkward: recognising the pecking order of authority didn't come naturally, either to those who did the saluting or to those who were supposed to receive the salutes.

It made sense that he'd been put in the cavalry unit, the Light Horse. And it made sense that Tom Chapel and Martin Jones should be placed there with him; they were good horsemen and good mates, they'd been at school together. At twelve years of age they all decided that they'd had enough education and went off to work in their family businesses or on the family farms – this was fairly standard practice around Ruby Hill. They'd remained close mates for the past seven years, so it was to be expected that, if one joined the recruitment march, then the other two would too. The other Ruby Hill lads who went through school with them didn't join the march. Ah, well.

Everyone, regardless of their unit, spent hours on horseback and hours on the rifle range. Competition between units and individuals was intense and encouraged by the officers who, like the enlisted men, weren't above laying a few quid on the results of an impromptu target shoot. The butt of most jokes were the blokes who'd been stuck in the artillery unit. Someone had forgotten to requisition any big guns for them to practise with. All they had was one old decommissioned cannon with open sights and its barrel full of concrete, and the same blokes were bloody useless on a horse and not much better with a .303.

Caring for your horse was sacrosanct. You could be reprimanded for your sloppy uniform, or your messy tent, or for not snapping off a salute to an officer, but you got seriously disciplined if you didn't look after your horse.

He gingerly stretched his left leg and tried to massage some feeling back into it, all the while being careful not to let his .303 scrape against the rocks and give his position away.

He missed his horse – Spinner he'd named him, from 'come in spinner' when you're playing two-up, and also because he used to spin away from you when you tried to get a foot in the stirrup. You ended up hopping around in circles like a bloody fool and his mates all laughed. Had to break him of that habit early on. Bloody beautiful little horse once they got to know each other.

Don't know what happened to Spinner. Had to leave him behind in Egypt when they embarked for the Dardanelles. Bloody ridiculous, train a bloke up as a cavalryman and then make him leave his horse behind when he went to fight, bloody ridiculous, probably a decision by some bloody stupid Pommy general drinking whisky in a club bar, bloody ridiculous.

He'd heard that Banjo Paterson was officer in charge of cavalry mounts. Damn good poet, Banjo. Their teacher back at Ruby Hill had made them memorise 'The man From Snowy River'. Martin Jones could recite it all the way through. He never could, but he remembered snatches of it. How did it go?

Clancy rode to wheel them – he was riding on the wing

Where the boldest riders took their place,
He raced his stockhorse past them,
and he made the ranges ring with his stockwhip.

Something like that. He'd look it up when he got home.

It was getting on for mid-morning but not getting any warmer. He was a bit exposed to the wind up here on the ridge. And getting bloody hungry – only brought a couple of biscuits and his canteen was only half-full, didn't expect to be up here for this long. He ate one of the biscuits and took a small swig from his canteen. His whole left side was getting numb. Bloody Turk should have shown himself by now.

The 'ocean cruise' began as a novelty for the Ruby Hill blokes. None of them had ever been on the open ocean or even been on a boat…er, ship. She was the HMAT *Orvieto* owned by the Orient Steam Navigation Company and leased to the Commonwealth. Not sure what the 'HMAT' stood for – something like 'His Majesty's Australian Transport' or maybe 'Army Transport'… Doesn't matter.

You could still see a few touches of the liner's former luxury, some walnut panelling here and there, a few fancy light fittings. But she'd just spent two months in the Sydney docks being refitted as a troop transport so it was all made functional. It had to be. They took on ninety officers and about thirteen hundred men with stores and horses for the first leg to King Georges Sound at Albany, where she was joined by a convoy of over thirty other ships. It was a bloody impressive sight.

The *Orvieto* was the biggest ship, with two tall funnels. Tom Chapel enjoyed looking down on some of the smaller ships and bombing them with oranges as they crept past. The time would come when he'd give his right arm for one of them oranges.

Conditions on board were cramped; you got allocated a canvas hammock which was only about two feet away from the next bloke's hammock. The atmosphere got mighty ripe at times and you either baked or froze. On the rare balmy nights, half of them tried to sleep up on deck; at least it wasn't so ripe.

The horses had it bad, nowhere to lie down: they spent the whole four weeks standing up and wedged together. The men spent half their time below decks mucking out the stalls and doing what they could for their horses, wetting them down when the heat got extreme, massaging their legs and necks. Sometimes, if the sea was calm and the boat wasn't pitching about, they could untie a horse and just back it in and out of the stall a few times just so's it got a bit of a stretch. Bloody awful!

The most interesting thing to happen was when the *Orvieto* was ordered to pick up German survivors of the *Emden*, a German raider that the HMAS *Sydney* had clobbered. They were the first enemy personnel that the Australians had seen, and they didn't look like much. Mind you, nobody would look like much after their ship had been bombarded and beached.

Then came the news that stunned everybody: Turkey had entered the war on the side of Germany. The implications unfolded bit by bit, none of them very welcome. Firstly, the AIF wouldn't be landing in England. This was a real bugger. Martin's great-uncle had a country estate near Dorchester, not far from the Salisbury army camp, and the three Ruby Hill recruits had planned on spending time there. A lot of soldiers had relatives in England, 'The Old Dart', and many of them were looking forward to social visits once they'd polished off the Hun, while they were still 'on holiday'.

Secondly, they were destined for Egypt, bloody Egypt! Very few Aussies knew anything about Egypt. Those who did reckoned that it was nothing but sand and Wogs. Oh, and mummies and pyramids.

The final days of the voyage were miserable, bloody hot and not much to look forward to.

Midday and a cold, misty rain looked to be settling in. Who'd have thought that it'd rain?

Still no sign of the Turk, no sign of any movement down there. Maybe he knew that someone was up here waiting for him. Surely not. He carefully laid down the heavy .303 and tried again to stretch his left leg but it was locked up. It sometimes did that; the docs reckoned that there were a few very small shards of bone floating around in his hip joint where the bullet had made a mess of things. Still, could be a lot worse – at least he still had two legs, even if the left one gave him gyp and he had to lean on a stick.

Leaving the rifle on the ridge, he slid himself slowly backwards away from his battlement until he was able to roll on his back, bend his knees and rotate his aching shoulders. It hurt like hell, especially his hips and left leg. His circulation brought stabbing pins and needles which were painful but sort of reassuring – he'd be all right for another hour or so.

Might as well knock off the last biscuit and wait for another hour or two. The bastard has to show his face sometime,

Egypt… The Poms hadn't made proper arrangements for the AIF's arrival. Men spent frigid nights sleeping on groundsheets in the open. Latrines were nothing but poles over communal pits.

The Ruby Hill trio and all of the Gunnedah recruits were eventually allocated tents at Maadi, the best of the three AIF camps not far out of Cairo. The horses were too fragile to be ridden; it took a month for them to become acclimatised and brought up to condition after the long voyage from Australia. They didn't know then that they'd be leaving their horses behind.

The men, other than when tending to the horses, found their days filled with endless drills, forced marches and target practice.

Whenever they got a day's leave, they headed into Cairo.

Cairo. Bloody hell! Never seen anything like it. The Blue Mosque was worth a look providing you didn't mind the bloody Wogs telling you how to behave, and the museum was interesting if you liked looking at dozens of dead bodies grinning at you or wrapped up in brown bandages.

But the people, the bloody Wogs! Strewth! Most of them were bloody filthy and had rotten teeth. The shopkeepers – well, if you could call them shops – were always trying to fleece a bloke. Their animals were all skinny-looking wretches. A lot of Aussie blokes got into trouble for flattening Wog blokes who were beating their horses with sticks. He'd snatched the stick off one Wog bloke and started beating him with it, really laying into the bastard. Martin and Tom had to pull him away and skedaddle before the coppers showed up.

And the...the loose women! Everywhere you looked there was some...some loose woman showing off her...her wares. There'd been lectures from the Pommy army medicos about the loose women, about the diseases that you'd likely get if you...if you fraternised with them, VD diseases they called them; showed us some bloody disgusting pictures too.

Still, plenty of blokes went ahead and...and fraternised. And a lot of them got a 'self-inflicted wound' and their pay was stopped while they went to hospital. Only one of the Gunnedah blokes got a 'self-inflicted wound'; he was sent off to the field hospital and when he came back we wouldn't let him sleep in our tent – might be contagious.

One of the officers came up with a name for the Aussie and Kiwi soldiers: ANZACS. We all thought that was bloody clever and someone wrote a song about it. How did it go again?

> We are the Anzac army, the Anzac,
> We cannot shoot, we don't salute. What bloody good are we?
> And when we get to Ber-lin the Kaiser he will say,
> '*Hoch, hoch! Mein Gott*, what a bloody lot to get six bob a day!

We had no instruments so made do with combs and tissue paper or bottle caps nailed onto broomsticks or gum leaves plucked from the groves of Eucalyptus trees planted a century earlier.

Yeah, funny how you remember some stupid things but forget other things.

The second of April was Good Friday but not all of the AIF observed it as a holy day; many of them headed into Cairo for a good time. One group, fed up with haggling with the locals, declared that they were being fleeced and started to push one of the shopkeepers around.

Within minutes, a full-blown punch-up developed and then it got out of hand.

The ensuing riot became known as the 'Battle of the Wazzer'. Houses and shops were burnt, three AIF soldiers were killed and others injured. The British command, by now fed up with the Anzacs' behaviour, declared Cairo to be out of bounds. This could have been enough provocation for the Anzacs, by now equally fed up with British command, to stage some sort of mutiny. Such insurgence was prevented when, within days, they received orders to embark for a secret, unknown destination, which everyone, on both sides, knew was to be Gallipoli.

The secrecy of the AIF's target was so poorly kept that the price of wheat in the USA dropped in anticipation of the opening up of the Dardanelles to Russian grain exports, The Turks knew, well in advance, that the invasion was coming. They were waiting,

Lance Corporal Winkie Williams pulled himself away from memories of Cairo and back to the sandstone ridge. He tried flexing his legs and shoulders to ease the cramp, his hip had locked up again and any movement was agony. The day was drawing to a close, sun getting low, and it was starting to feel very cold, soon be dusk.

Still no sign of the bloody Turk. He'd have to decide whether to maintain the vigil or give it away for the day and head for home. Maybe another half-hour...

Sometime after three in the morning, the invading Anzacs clambered down the slack rope ladders and into the rowboats, bloody hard work with all the stuff they had to carry, full uniform, rifles, ammo, grenades, water, rucksacks,

The three Ruby Hill and the Gunnedah soldiers were all packed into the same rowboat with a dozen others. Then each boat was hooked up to one of the little steamers to tow them on to the beach. Dawn was just breaking, getting lighter. As they approached the beach, there were boats all around and the Turks were starting to lay it on from their vantages above the steep slopes behind the beach, machine guns, rifles and some heavy stuff. The boat next to Winkie's copped a direct hit and blokes were thrown into the sea; some were screaming, everyone was shouting.

Several of the big, heavy rowboats came together with a loud splintering of timbers, a couple of blokes, thinking that they'd wade ashore, jumped out and were immediately dragged under by the weight of their kit.

One of Winkie's memories was of the water around the boat and how it reminded him of how the first fat raindrops of an approaching storm would strafe the surface of the creek, each drop raising a little column of water. Then he realised that these raindrops were Turk bullets.

He remembered a scream right next to him and one of the Gunnedah boys grabbing at his shoulder. Then something punched him heavily in his left side. He looked down and there was blood, torn fabric and blood. And then, as he looked down in bemused fascination, there was another thud, and more torn fabric further down, in his thigh, and more blood.

And then there was a lot more screaming from all around him. Blokes were writhing in the bottom of the boat. And some of the screaming was his own because the pain of his wounds had just reached his brain. And he remembered feeling a raging, bitter anger. 'Bugger, all the drills, and the marches, and the training, all the trouble it took to get here, and I'm not going to be shooting any Turks. Bastards.'

And then something heavy smacked against the back of his head and the rest of the Anzac landing was lost to him,

He was wounded but he wasn't one of the two thousand troops who died on that first day nor one of the eight thousand Australians who died during the eight-month struggle; he was one of the few who, unconscious and bleeding heavily, was taken back to one of only a handful of ships that had a doctor on board.

Many of his wounded compatriots found themselves evacuated to ships with no medical facilities. There they lay in filthy conditions until infection either killed them or intensified their injuries.

It was also rather ironic that Winkie's shattered hip ruled out an automatic amputation. Shattered knees and feet usually meant a quick amputation and primitive cauterisation of the stump. But the hip? Well, where does a doctor, with no real surgical equipment other than a scalpel and a bone saw, amputate a hip? So Winkie's doctor probed around until he'd removed the shrapnel and the more obvious bone fragments and then dosed the wound in alcohol and stitched him up. Then he stitched up the small flesh wound in his thigh, bandaged the split in his scalp where a broken oar had smacked him and told the orderlies to lie him down on deck alongside scores of other wounded. Then he proceeded to remove an arm from his next patient.

Lance Corporal Winkie Williams was evacuated back to the hospital in Cairo. He was one of hundreds who, once it was decided that they might survive their wounds, were moved to a makeshift hospital ward under tarpaulins stretched over a nearby tennis court. It was there that the first indications that his minor head wound might not be as minor as first thought.

The boat trip from Gallipoli to Cairo had been hellish – not so much the voyage itself but the transfers from rowboat to ship, to shore, and then to hospital. He was strapped to a stretcher which was hauled, cargo-style, scraping up and down the hull of the ship. There was no available morphine on board to ease the pain caused by the strappings or the excruciating, searing agony brought on by the slightest bump. The pain was intensified by his raging anger and frustration: he'd come here to kill Turks, the whole purpose of the campaign was to kill Turks. And now he was being shoved around, trussed, like a bloody Turkish goat.

He still had all four limbs, unlike most of the poor buggers who lay around him, legs missing, arms hacked off, half of them moaning and groaning, losing their sanity. But he was complete…well, he couldn't walk yet, couldn't even sit up, but a couple of weeks in Cairo and he'd be patched up enough to rejoin his mates at Gallipoli, shooting bastard Turks, providing his mates hadn't polished off the bastards before he got back.

Somewhere, born within the befogged stupor of his pain, the morphine, the reluctant realisation of his uselessness and the obsessive loathing of all things Turkish, came the confusion of Egyptians with Turks. The bastard that had been beating his horse with a stick, the one that he'd beaten with his own stick before Martin and Tom pulled him away, became, because he was a filthy, disgusting shit, a Turk, because Turks were filthy and disgusting and beat their animals and their women with sticks, because…

And then there were bloody Turkish hospital orderlies, here, in this hospital where he was stuck, and one of the bastards wanted to wash him and change his dressings, a bloody Turk! Right here, just like that bastard that he'd beaten with a stick. Should have shot the bastard while he'd had the chance. Have to get out of this hospital and shoot some Turks, because…

He'd lunged at the little Egyptian orderly, grabbed his arm and tried to pull him close enough to get a grip on his throat. The dismayed Egyptian had instinctively pulled away dragging the patient with him. Lance Corporal Winkie Williams had ended up on the floor, screaming obscenities and bleeding heavily from his reopened wound. Even on the floor he'd lashed out at the two nurses who'd tried to help him.

They eventually got him strapped to a bed and the doctor stitched him up again while, all the time, Winkie kept screaming obscenities and threats that he'd shoot any Turk that came near him. Assurances that there weren't any Turks within a thousand miles were met with incoherent snarls. Eventually they administered a dose of their precious morphine and he passed out.

The Egyptian orderlies continued to be the target for the invective shouted from his bed; in his addled brain they were still Turks. When the nurses removed the restraining straps from his bed, he crawled across the tennis-court-hospital-ward and used the steel mesh to pull himself to a standing position. He needed to show the doctors that he was fit to return to Gallipoli, fit to shoot Turks. It didn't work – the pain beat him and, again, he needed a dose of morphine and more stitches replaced.

After enduring three weeks of their patient's bellowing paranoia, the hospital staff quietly celebrated his transfer to an Australia-bound return convoy. No one regretted his removal, not the doctors and nurses nor the scores of wounded men, and certainly not the Egyptian orderlies who were neither horse-beaters nor wife-abusers, nor Turks. They were Coptic Christians and they were Red Cross volunteers.

He was quiet and calm as they carried him aboard the *Ascanius*. He'd got it into his head that the ship was going to carry him back to Gallipoli, to his mates, and the Turks. Most likely someone had put that idea into his head, possibly a doctor or a nurse, more probably an Egyptian orderly. By agreement, they'd kept him below decks, away from the portholes and dosed with morphine as they crept through the Suez Canal. It wasn't until the convoy was well into the Khalij as-Suways, the Gulf of Suez, that Winkie realised that he'd been hoodwinked, that he was being carried further away from any chance that he might have had of shooting a Turk.

Captain Westfield took his binoculars from the binnacle, stepped out on to *Ascanius*'s minuscule flying bridge, and slowly swept the horizon on the seaward side. Then he quartered the waters fore and aft according to the Royal Navy's protocols. His wasn't a Royal Navy craft and Captain Westfield, built like a short, bald bollard, didn't fit the Royal Navy mould. But it made sense to follow their methods. Too many merchant ships had suffered the consequences of lax watch-keeping. Satisfied that the *Ascanius* was on station within the convoy he crossed the bridge and stepped out on the port side.

They were about twelve nautical miles offshore, so he had a clear view of the desolate coast, not much of a view. The first mate was leaning on the binnacle when his captain stepped back in to the bridge.

He took the binoculars. 'Anything?'

'Nothing. What a God-forsaken stretch of coast.' The first mate was his captain's physical opposite: tall, slim, bespectacled and scholarly, as unlikely a seaman, or officer, as might be found in any navy. He raised the binoculars to study the shoreline, mostly sand dunes with untidy fishing villages every mile or so. 'Some of those little communities can claim ancestral links to the ancient tribes of Gebadaei and the Autaci,' he said to no one in particular.

The helmsman, a bored-looking Welshman, found little interest in this historical peanut.

The captain, who had ceased to be surprised at his first mate's eclectic knowledge, nodded as if he too was au fait with the ancient tribes of Gebadaei and the Autaci. 'I wonder if they can hear that noisy bastard on the fantail,' he muttered.

'Noisy bastard,' echoed the helmsman, and then went back to looking dead ahead and dead bored.

By the time the *Ascanius* had cleared the Khalij as-Suways and entered the Al-Bahr Al-ahmar, the Red Sea, everybody was ready to chuck Lance Corporal Winkie Williams overboard. His incessant and incoherent ramblings had gone beyond the point of being annoying, had gone beyond the point of getting on everyone's nerves, had reached the point where it espoused a dunking.

The captain, fearing an onboard murder, or an overboard murder, or, truth be told, fearing the irksome enquiries subsequent to an onboard murder, or, truth be further told, an onboard murder that he had personally committed, ordered Winkie to be moved as far away from the bridge as was possible given the limited deck space. So it was that Winkie found himself isolated on the fantail, the poop, alone and surrounded by a canvas screen.

Even here, remote from everyone, he continued to be a bloody nuisance. There is a phenomenon known as 'The dripping tap effect'. You are lying in bed, seeking sleep, when you hear a tap dripping into the kitchen sink. It gets louder, you cover your head with a pillow, it's till audible. You turn on your bedside radio, still there.

So it was aboard the *Ascanius*. No matter where you were or what you were doing, you could still hear Winkie's incessant complaining. The captain on the bridge heard him, the stokers in the very bowels of the ship imagined that they could hear him above the din of the boiler and engine. Of course they couldn't, just like the dripping tap can't really be heard. But it's the knowing, the knowing that it's still dripping.

As it turned out, no one threw Winkie overboard. There wasn't the need. Winkie suddenly fell broodingly silent. And it was Charlie 'Churchie' Chapel, one of those stokers who regularly popped up from the boiler room for a quick fag, who was responsible.

Charlie ChurchieChapel hailed from Narrabri. A cousin to Tom Chapel, one of Winkie's fellow recruits from Ruby Hill, so he'd known Winkie for years, played cricket against him, they'd caught yabbies together when he'd come down from Narrabri on family visits.

Churchie had strolled onto the ship's fantail, his usual spot for a surreptitious fag, only to find a canvas screen had been erected and that 'Whingeing Winkie' was lying and whingeing within. The stoker, unhappy at finding his quiet refuge occupied, had put his head around the canvas screen with the intention of offering the whinger a few words of advice, something along the lines of 'Why don't you shut up, you stupid bastard?' To his amazement, he recognised his Ruby Hill mate and immediately enquired, 'Why don't you shut up, you stupid bastard?' It was the inflexion on the 'bastard' that gave the comment an entirely new tenor.

They talked for an hour. At one point, the angry chief engineer came looking to drag that 'lazy bloody Australian' back to shovelling coal. Then the captain, worried by the sudden silence, came to check that Winkie hadn't gone for an assisted dive off the poop deck. Both tiptoed away from the canvas screen and left the two men to their chat, and both agreed that Churchie could absent himself from the boiler for as long as he kept the whingeing patient quiet.

It was towards the end of the hour that the two newly reunited friends started to reminisce about Narrabri and Ruby Hill, about friends in common, about local sport, about any news that they'd had from home, about how good it was going to be to get home to friends and family, people they'd left behind. It was during these reflections that another notion, clad in a cloak of black guile, crept into Winkie's head to rekindle the sparks of obsession and fan the flames of paranoia.

It was as they spoke of Narrabri and Ruby Hill, and their friends, the people back home. He remembered that not all of the young men of Ruby Hill had enlisted, a few had resisted the cooee marches and the romantic stories of fighting men and the appeals to patriotism and loyalty to the Old Country. A few young fellers had opted to stay home.

Many volunteers spat contempt for the stay-at-home non-enlisters, branded them as cowards and bludgers. Winkie hadn't given these blokes a second thought or, if he had, it was because he'd felt sorry for them: they'd missed the opportunity for travel to exotic places with a bunch of mates, the opportunity to fight for King and Country, the opportunity to shoot Turks.

But now, since his wounding at the Gallipoli landing, he'd come to despise those craven weaklings, those young blokes who'd stayed behind in Ruby Hill. He started to list them in his head. There was Clem Pridham, but he'd got something wrong with his back, that was why he couldn't play footy. There was Reg Tonkin, he lived on a farm just out of Ruby Hill, he could've joined up if he'd really wanted to. There was Michael-Mehmet Demir, Michael-Mehmet Demir…and it was with the remembering of Michael-Mehmet Demir that Lance Corporal Winkie Williams forgot about the rest of Ruby Hill's non-enlisters, because his head filled with thoughts of Michael-Mehmet Demir, and his resolve became…resolved.

The Demirs could trace their ancestry back through centuries but very little of it happened in Australia – all but sixty-odd years had happened in Akhisar, in Turkey. Michael-Mehmet's grandfather, just plain Mehmet without any hyphenated adjunct, had arrived in Melbourne in the 1850s as a crew member on a clipper. No one knew why he'd become a sailor; there weren't many Turkish sailors on British boats back then because most of Europe still had a deep distrust of anything Ottoman, except couches, which were fashionably acceptable.

There was some talk about *Büyük bab*, grandfather Mehmet, having to flee from Akhisar in the dead of night to escape the wrath of certain men who wanted to settle a score. No one ever said what score needed settling – could have been money, could have been a feud, could have been…well, family legend has it that *Büyük baba* Mehmet was a man of vigour when he was younger, before he became a *Büyük baba*, a grandfather.

Family legend also has it that he jumped ship and joined the hundreds of hopefuls heading for the goldfields, where no one spoke his language and he spoke none of theirs. So he never understood the need for a miner's licence, or how to stake a claim, or how to go about finding gold or how to go about surviving in the bush. But *Büyük baba* Mehmet Demir was no fool. He did a clever thing: he married a recently widowed lady, Margaret, who ran a small general store in Ballarat.

Taking gold from miners in exchange for groceries was a lot easier that digging it up for yourself and the newly wed Demirs built up a nice little nest egg before the entrepreneurial Chinese opened their own stores and planted their own vegetable gardens and stole most of their customers.

When Margaret announced an expected addition to their union, they decided that it was time to quit the primitive, unsanitary and unruly goldfields. They used their savings to buy a better life in Gunnedah, where there were neither gold, nor ratbag miners, nor entrepreneurial Chinese. By the time baby Martin-Mehmet Demir arrived, they'd purchased the Gunnedah general store with attached residence and a few acres on the Namoi River, where they established a commercial vegetable garden.

The village of Gunnedah grew into a prosperous town as more wealthy graziers arrived with their flocks of sheep and herds of cows. The Demirs' small general store became a large general store and diversified with mail contracts and bank agencies.

In time, young Martin-Mehmet Demir, having exhausted the limited educational opportunities on offer in Gunnedah, was packed off to Sydney's premier boarding school. Within four years of his return, he became manager of the family's newly opened branch in Ruby Hill, married a local pastoralist's daughter and became father to Michael-Mehmet Demir.

Young Michael-Mehmet Demir attended the tiny Ruby Hill primary school along with Len Williams, Tom Chapel, Martin Jones and a handful of other lads and lasses. His hyphenated name, being too much of a mouthful for his mates, was reduced to Mike. They all played sport together, they all got up to mischief together, they all left school at the end of grade seven and joined their family's businesses, farming, fencing, general storekeeping and the like.

The Demirs were well-liked in Ruby Hill. Their general store became one of the social centres of town, the other one being the pub. When the locals referred to them as 'the Turks', there was no hint of racism; no, it was said as a term of humorous friendship, so much so that the attractive Mrs Demir fell into character by whipping up big batches of Turkish delight and giving small cubes of it, dusted with icing sugar, to each and every customer whenever they made a purchase. Young Mike's access to the offcuts of his mum's Turkish delight certainly enhanced his popularity with his mates.

There were few in Ruby Hill or Gunnedah who knew, or cared, about the increasingly closer ties that had been forged between Germany and Turkey since the Russo-Turkish War of the 1870s. These were the sort of international conspiracies, the sort of foreign affairs, that held the interest of Australia's federal politicians but they definitely weren't discussion topics in either the Demirs' general store or the pub.

And as for the Demirs…well, good-natured locals may have called them 'the Turks' but there were none who, in their wildest inventions, made any connection between the Demirs and anything German. It was a long way from Turkish delight to sauerkraut.

He tried twisting his hips to get some feeling back into his legs but the pain that shot up through his back almost made him cry out. He bit his bottom lip, face pressed into the crook of his elbow; no point spending bloody hours up here and then give his position away by making a noise.

Once again, he slid slowly back from his battlement until he was out of sight of anyone who might be looking up. Gingerly he rolled onto his back and, by using his elbows, was able to push himself into a sitting position. An involuntary gasp escaped him as his left hip resisted before finally clicking into place. That's all right; no one would hear him, he was far enough below the ridge.

It felt better to be sitting up. Every cramped joint and muscle was a tingling ache as circulation returned, not entirely unpleasant, a bit like pulling a bandage off a wound, hurt like hell while it was happening but a wonderful relief once it was off.

The bloody rain was definitely settling in, heavy enough to start soaking right through his clothes, bloody annoying, and enough to make the dirt slippery and colder. He wished now that he'd had the foresight to bring a groundsheet and an overcoat. He'd started shivering. Difficult to aim a .303 when you're shivering. Bloody rain, bloody Turk.

Bloody hungry now; the last biscuit gone. Reminiscing about the endless supply of Turkish delight that Mike brought to every escapade didn't help.

Mike, Michael-bloody-Mehmet-bloody-Demir, bloody Turk.

Always one of the gang, going to school together, playing cricket, just like every other bloke in Ruby Hill. Well, he'd had us all fooled, him and his mum and his dad. Everyone called them 'the Turks', smiling when they said it, just like everyone called Martin Jones's dad 'Pommy Pete', didn't really mean everything, just a friendly nickname back then.

It wasn't until they were on the boat to Egypt that he started to hear about how the Germans and the Turks had been getting awfully friendly. Apparently been going on for years, armies training together, building railways. God knows what else they'd been up to. Didn't hear about all these goings-on back in Ruby Hill…well, not many locals heard about it, but he'd bet that the Demirs knew all about it, and kept it under their hats. No wonder Michael-bloody-Mehmet-bloody-Demir didn't join the recruitment march when it came through Ruby Hill; he'd snuck off somewhere. No wonder he never joined up later; didn't want to point a gun at his own kind, bloody Turk. We thought that he'd just been a bit gutless, now we all know that he was a bloody traitorous Turk all along.

He crawled back up to his vantage point, wiped the moisture from the .303 and pulled his hat lower over his eyes. The evening was getting noticeably duller, and a hell of a lot colder, the rain a bit heavier. Doesn't matter; he could put up with a couple of hours of discomfort. There was a bloody Turk down there, and he was going to shoot him.

'That's him?' asked Ray Dunn. Although there couldn't be much doubt. Not a lot of blokes went missing, and not many warranted a search party. Ray had volunteered two days ago, one of a dozen blokes who'd been organised into pairs and given an area to walk through. He'd been paired with Trev, who was a lot older, lived around Ruby Hill for most of his life so he knew the ground pretty well.

'Yeah, that's him,' answered Trevor Lister. 'That's Len, that's Winkie.' He knelt down and went through the motions of looking for a pulse but they both knew that it was a token search. Winkie was stiff and motionless, curled up as if against the cold. He looked very small and fragile. The big .303 rifle, hugged against his chest, made him look smaller. 'Silly old bugger.'

'Any sign of how he died?'

'Not obvious. Could be a heart attack, probably exposure. He's not dressed well enough to have been out here overnight, two nights.'

'What's he doing up here anyway? Nothing around here, just the old farm on the other side of the ridge but no one's lived there for years. Was he hunting?'

Trevor straightened up. 'Yeah, you could say that – hunting.' He took the four steps to look down to the other side of the ridge. 'That place used to belong to Mike Demir.' He turned to Ray. 'Did you know Mike Demir? Used to run the general store here. Family's got the big store and vegetable farm in Gunnedah. Mike moved back there when his old man died, sold the Ruby Hill store to the Lees, you know, the Chinese couple?'

'Yeah, I know the Chinese, they seem all right. Don't know about Mike Demir, before my time. What's this got to do with Len Williams?' asked Ray, glancing down at the cold body and then away again.

'Len, Winkie, was wounded at Gallipoli. Came back very disturbed, a bit insane. Had it in his head that the Demirs were Turks and that it was his job to shoot them, especially young Mike because he hadn't joined up with Len and some other young lads from Ruby Hill.'

'Bloody hell.'

'Yeah. He was laid up in Sydney for a few months with some serious wounds. First thing we knew that he was back in Ruby Hill was when he opened fire on the store, put about ten rounds through the front door and windows before the copper clobbered him with his stick.'

'Bloody hell.'

'The cops charged him with all kinds of felonies, attempted

murder, endangering public safety and suchlike. Turned out that Winkie was off his rocker, deranged, a real nutcase. So they locked him up in the loony bin. Been locked up for all this time until he just walked out three days ago. Don't know where he got that .303 – must have had it buried somewhere all along. Looks like he's been up here for a couple of days, waiting to get a shot at Mike Demir.

'But you said that Mike Demir was in Gunnedah.'

'That's right, he is, but Winkie couldn't have known that. Winkie's world has been locked into 1915 ever since Gallipoli.'

'But Gallipoli? I mean that was…how long ago?'

'About fifty years, give or take. Time to have another world war since then.'

'So how old is this Winkie?' Again, a quick glance at the body.

'Well, figure it out. Late sixties, I suppose.'

'And ever since the First World War he's been locked up in an asylum and planning to shoot Mike Demir?'

'Yeah, the nearest available Turk.'

'Bloody hell.'